Iain halted be[...]

'Enjoy your lunch,' [...] his hand brushing a[...] ~~~~ giving her a light pat on the shoulder. Surprised into catching her breath, she jerked backwards and it seemed as if her head would have impulsively rested against his chest had he not hurried off.

Now what did he have to touch me for? she asked herself angrily, hoping he had not read more into her surprised reaction than that it was an impulsive and natural response to being taken off-guard, and nothing more than that. . .

Dear Reader

Nature gets its own back this month! Stella Whitelaw's DELUGE takes us to the dangerous waters of the North Sea, and Meredith Webber's WHISPER IN THE HEART includes a terrifying bush fire! There's water in HEARTS AT SEA by Clare Lavenham, following a cruise ship, but STILL WATERS—despite the title!—by Kathleen Farrell brings us to earth in Edinburgh. All good stuff for you to enjoy.

The Editor

!!!STOP PRESS!!! If you enjoy reading these medical books, have you ever thought of writing one? We are always looking for new writers for LOVE ON CALL, and want to hear from you. Send for the guidelines, and start writing!

Kathleen Farrell was born in South Africa, but the family settled in England while she was still a child. After working in a bank, she volunteered for the WAAFS and worked on the then highly-secret British radar defence system. She married and brought up five children while working as a freelance journalist. Her daughter is a hospital surgeon who enjoys helping Kathleen with the medical background to her stories.

Recent titles by the same author:

THE SINGAPORE AFFAIR
NO TIME FOR ROMANCE
A STORMY PARTNERSHIP

STILL WATERS

BY
KATHLEEN FARRELL

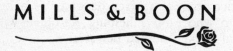

MILLS & BOON LIMITED
ETON HOUSE, 18-24 PARADISE ROAD
RICHMOND, SURREY TW9 1SR

To Maryanne, for her never-failing help

*MILLS & BOON, the Rose Device and LOVE ON CALL
are trademarks of the publisher.*

*First published in Great Britain 1994
by Mills & Boon Limited*

© *Kathleen Farrell 1994*

*Australian copyright 1994   Philippine copyright 1994
This edition 1994*

ISBN 0 263 78757 5

Set in Times 11 on 12 pt.

03-9409-41752

Made and printed in Great Britain

CHAPTER ONE

HURRYING into her flat, undressing there and washing away all the stains of blood, Mary put on her finest lingerie, smartest suit, quickly applied make-up then rushed to the Royal Glen Hospital.

Knowing herself almost too late for her interview, she was very relieved to have the attending personnel officer immediately accept her apologies and gabbled excuses, and simply point her to the one remaining empty chair in the small waiting area.

'I didn't think I'd make it in time,' Mary said breathlessly to the young man she found herself sitting beside. 'I've been busy since dawn seeing to that poor local lad injured in an RTA. Life's all hustle and bustle, isn't it?' she ran on. 'I don't suppose I stand a chance of getting the "staff-grade doctor" job going vacant here. I only applied because the shorter hours and unlikelihood of being called out at night tempted me.'

'You have home ties?' the young man stirred himself to ask.

'Twins.'

'And you want to be able to spend more time with them?'

'Naturally.'

'Very commendable,' he murmured in a pre-occupied way, no doubt thinking of his own coming interview which was due to follow hers. 'How many selectors are there on the board, do you know?' he asked next, adding, 'I'm Andrew Buchan, by the way.'

'Mary Macgregor.' Half-smiling but still puffing a little, she shook the proffered hand and replied, 'From what I've heard, there should be three selectors, namely the accident and emergency consultant, the senior orthopaedic consultant, and a member of the public, someone without any connection whatsoever with the hospital, more probably a boss of some big business concern.'

She took a deep breath, sighed, fiddled with the strap of her shoulder-bag then suddenly stopped. 'I'd better keep my fingers still while being interviewed. Wouldn't do to give the impression that I'm lacking in confidence. Signs like that are watched out for, aren't they?'

Andrew quickly removed his hands from where he had stuck them deep into his pockets and self-consciously straightened his tie.

'The A and E consultant is quite impressive,' Mary ran on. 'A tall rugger-built type, very serious, views the world through a frown. . .or is that only when I'm around?' She shrugged. 'Maybe I imagine it? He's probably hardly aware that I exist!'

At that moment a secretary came out of a nearby doorway calling 'Mrs Mary Macgregor?'

'Mrs?' Andrew was stunned. 'Married. . .also a mother, and with a surgical fellowship too? My, you've been busy!'

Mary's answering look was a little sad. 'I've

had to be,' she declared wearily. 'Besides, I don't believe in wasting time. . . Life's much too short for that.'

'But a surgeon. . .and you so slight too!'

'Deceptively meek and weak, that's me! Anyway, wish me luck.' Bending, Mary elbowed him to further ensure his attention, suddenly needing extra support, then, tense and with colour beginning to drain from her cheeks, 'I've got to get this job, simply got to!' she stressed.

Tightly clenching her even white teeth in an effort to bolster herself up, and determinedly walking as tall as her five feet three inches would allow, Mary suppressed off the fear that she was fighting an already lost cause and followed the secretary into the room set aside for the interviews.

'Good morning!' The three men sitting behind the long table greeted her, obviously taking careful note of the way she held herself, and especially her composure when sitting down facing them.

Then, to her relief, they seemed to concentrate on her curriculum vitae lying on the desk before them.

Several medically based questions followed, Mary gaining confidence because she had no difficulty in answering correctly.

But suddenly, quite without warning, the A and E consultant, Mr Iain Stewart, shot a bolt from the blue.

'I see that you have two small sons,' he muttered, looking down at his notes. 'Might I ask what guarantee you can give us that you would not prove unreliable because of having to look after them?'

Mary's Scottish-blue eyes glinted like cold steel. 'It is against Government guidelines to ask that at an interview,' she pointed out, anger chasing away diffidence. 'After all, if I felt unable to give all necessary attention to both the children and the job, I would not be applying,' she added indignantly.

The three men glanced at one another and Mary's face was not the only one to bear a sudden heated flush. Iain Stewart's was positively blazing!

The interview ending abruptly, Mary was ushered outside to await the board's decision.

'I blew it!' she muttered to Andrew who was the next, and last, to be interviewed. 'My stupid fault. I shouldn't have answered back, but the A and E consultant stung me. Still, you might be luckier.'

'Mr Andrew Buchan?' called the secretary, waiting to lead him before the board. Then, his turn over, all the candidates were called back in again, one after another, to be told the final decision, Iain Stewart acting as spokesman for the board.

When Mary faced him again she was sure he scowled at her. Nevertheless, 'You have been chosen for the job on a majority vote,' he said, although with such an air of reluctance that it seemed clear he had not voted for her himself, especially when he muttered, 'My only hope is that you will prove me wrong.'

So she was very surprised when he added in a

low voice, 'You were right, I should not have asked what I did,' when giving her the customary congratulatory handshake, and, looking up at him, she saw the semblance of an apologetic smile on his otherwise impassive face.

Slightly dazed, but remembering to express her thanks to the other board members, Mary walked from the room.

'You failed?' Andrew studied her puzzled face with some sympathy as she again took the seat beside him.

'No, believe it or not, I've been given the job. The only thing is I'll be working under the inexplicable Mr Stewart and I can't make him out at all. We've had a few brushes in the past when both attending the same regional casualty meetings, so I know he disapproves of some of my medical methods just as I disagree with some of his, but just now he acted so out of character. . .it got me completely fogged!'

'He certainly seems to have upset you—that's rotten!' Andrew patted her head sympathetically while rising to go and hear his own fate.

He came back, unable to hide his satisfaction. 'I've been given a job too,' he declared elatedly. 'It's because of my former experience in orthopaedics. Seems a registrar-locum is needed soon for four months as the present orthopaedic registrar has been promoted, so I'll be starting work on August first, and with the possibility of getting on to a rotation afterwards.'

'That's great!' Mary raised a warm smile, genuinely pleased, having taken a liking to Andrew

from the first moment they met. He reached out
to help her from her chair.

'Thanks for waiting for me; I hoped you would,'
he smiled. 'Are you in a hurry or can you come and
have a celebratory lunch with me somewhere?'

Grateful for the calming effect he had had upon
her troubled spirits, 'I'd like that,' she said, standing up and glancing at her watch. 'My child-minder
leaves at three-thirty, so I've got time.'

'Child-minder?' Andrew raised an enquiring
eyebrow while walking her out of the impressive
hospital façade. Then, distracted from what he
had been about to ask, he pointed ahead. 'Ah,
look, there's a restaurant on the other side of the
square; shall we try it?' he suggested.

'Why not?' Mary replied promptly. 'I'm starving! Let's go Dutch, then I can choose what I like
without considering your pocket.'

'Suits me; I'd forgotten about the big hole in
my pocket!'

'How come a big hole? What have you
been up to?'

'Nothing criminal! I simply took a year off and
travelled around Australia and New Zealand.'
Escorting her into the small restaurant, Andrew
led the way to a table for two. 'Did odd jobs,
very odd, some of them,' he continued, 'barely
managing to scrape a living at times.'

'So what are you going to have now?' Mary
studied the printed menu left lying on the glass-
topped table. 'Water and dry bread?'

'I'm not quite that impoverished,' he grinned.
'Soup and a roll, perhaps.' He hid the menu

out of his sight as if to resist temptation.

Mary chuckled, noticing but refusing to show any pity or feel sorry for him.

'Are you on the dole too?' he asked.

'No. I'm an SHO in Edinburgh's small Florence Nightingale Hospital, A and E department. I wanted this Royal Glen staff-grade job for many reasons, mostly personal, also because, although I wanted to get out of the rat-race towards consultantship, I'm as ambitious as the next person and eager to be on a permanent contract with a hospital. Not many doctors in hospitals can claim to be permanent, only consultants and staff-grade doctors; most others have to seek new appointments every six months, as you obviously must know.'

'Soup of the day and a roll, no butter,' Andrew said firmly to the waitress coming up notepad in hand and waiting for orders.

'Battered haddock, chips and peas, bread and butter and tea,' ordered Mary, adding to Andrew, when the waitress had left, 'You can share my bread and butter if you like, or even some of the rest?'

'No, thanks—sweet of you but no, thanks, I'm content to suffer.' He grinned. 'I can't accept charity—my pride won't allow it! No, I don't mean that; however, it won't hurt me to starve for a few weeks.' Humorously he pulled a long, self-pitying face. 'I've back-rent to pay which will probably use up all my dole.'

'Ah, I hear violins!' Mary mocked gently.

He laughed. 'You've no soul!' he chided. 'All

the same, I'll treat you to a proper lunch when I get my first month's salary from the hospital.'

'I'll hold you to that,' Mary said seriously, 'that's if I can find you; the Glen seems all corridors!'

'Then look for me in those leading to the lost property department,' he suggested facetiously. 'Now, what was that about a child-minder. . .? Why do you have one? Can't relatives help?'

Debating how to answer, Mary poured tomato sauce without really seeing it, covering all the chips and peas as well as the haddock.

'Did you mean to do that?' Andrew questioned, screwing up his short nose at the distasteful sight.

'No, I was miles away, thinking of my twins and how I miss them every second I'm away from them.' She saddened. 'I wish I didn't have to leave them at all, but I have no family to call on now that my Dad's had to join his regiment in Germany, and has taken Mother with him.

'Mind you,' she added thoughtfully, 'Debbie-Ann, my child-minder, is very good and the boys like her a lot. I don't think they miss me much when she's there. She's more than a child-minder really, more of an au pair and friend than anything. The trouble is, she comes from Cape Town and longs to visit her parents, her father not being too well. I don't quite know what to do about it. I know she's worrying about him and longing to see him so that she can judge his condition for herself, but on the other hand she's reluctant to leave me in the lurch with the twins to see to as well as my job.'

'I see,' Andrew muttered, breaking open his roll. 'Good, it's crusty. I hate those soft ones.' He tackled the soup. 'And this isn't at all bad either.'

He ate rather hungrily for a minute or two, leaving Mary wondering whether he had had anything to eat that morning. Then he looked up to add, 'You know, I can't imagine you being a mum; you seem so young, even carefree at times.'

'As I was, once.' Mary's face became strained again as she looked back into the past. 'I married a year before graduation, then my husband was sent on a peacekeeping mission overseas—he was an army officer like my Dad. In fact that's how we met, Dad introducing us. My parents were happy to have me marry him.'

Her mouth lost its usual upward curve. 'Then Robert got in the way of a sniper's bullet— inaccurately aimed, I like to think,' she sighed heavily and her voice dropped. 'Unfortunately, for him that was that. For me too, in a way.'

'Oh, I'm sorry.' Andrew looked very uncomfortable, no doubt wishing he had not brought up the subject.

Mary got to her feet, leaving most of her lunch. 'I must go,' she said, brushing away the tear escaping down her cheek and adding a wry, 'I hate getting emotional in public, don't you?'

Reaching over the table, she scribbled a number on the paper serviette beside him. 'That's my phone number,' she explained hurriedly. And with a rushed, 'Cheerio,' she left the café, biting her lips hard to control her roused unhappiness, talk of her husband having reopened the door to her private anguish.

Later, having changed into casual clothes, she collected the twins from their playschool. Taking them to a playground in a park and buying ice-creams all round, she found comfort in just being with the boys and seeing them enjoying themselves.

Only one thing was to spoil the fun. A car stopped beside them as they left the park, the driver calling out of an open window to offer them a lift. Mary took one look and mentally shuddered. 'No thank you, we enjoy walking,' she said proudly.

'And limping?' Iain Stewart asked caustically. 'One of the boys limps quite badly.'

'Oh, does he? I hadn't noticed.' Picking up the three-and-a-half-year-old, Mary sat on the kerb with him to examine his feet. 'There doesn't seem to be anything wrong,' she muttered, a little on the defensive because Iain Stewart still peered from his open window, leaving her feeling ill at ease, before—giving her a look which she decided was so imperturbable that anyone could read just about anything into it—he drove off.

She stood up, lifting the twin with her, his chubby legs straddling her waist.

'I doesn't do what he says I does,' he grizzled, tugging at the neck of her black tunic top to keep his balance.

'He didn't know you were only playing.' Clasping his hands, she let him slide down her Macgregor tartan leggings to the pavement. 'But don't any more or you'll twist your feet and I'll have to buy you more shoes instead of the car I'll be buying for us soon.'

It was no idle promise. When a permanent staff-grade doctor she would be able to feel secure about taking out loans for things like cars, thought Mary, whereas, while having to find new hospital jobs every six months, the insecurity forbade the taking up of any extra financial risks, especially when one had children to support.

'I fink I'm all right now,' said Rob—or was it Richie? Even Mary had difficulty in distinguishing between her identical twins at times, especially when their faces weren't visible, as now when whichever one it was turned turtle upon reaching ground level.

'I thought you wouldn't manage to carry him for long,' said Iain's deep voice as they turned the corner, 'which was why I waited.'

The two little boys instantly raced to tug at the door-handles, determined not to let the car get away again without them having a ride in it first.

'Where do you live?' Iain asked Mary.

'Wasn't my address down in your notes?' she queried irritably.

'"Mary, Mary, quite contrary,"' he quoted, 'I can see why you were given that name! Come on, don't be stubborn. I'll drop you home.'

A canny look crept into Mary's eyes. 'All right, if you insist,' she said, getting into the back of the car with the boys. 'Turn off into Beech Grove,' she directed. 'I'll tell you where to stop.'

'Beech Grove?' He sounded surprised.

She remained silent, an imp of mischief taking

hold again, then suddenly she called, 'Here we are, please stop!'

Iain glanced at the large ornate double gates at the entrance to a drive leading to an elegant mansion. He seemed impressed. 'The family home?' he asked. 'Can you manage the walk up the drive?'

'No problem,' declared Mary, enforcing an abrupt exodus upon her struggling sons, who wanted to remain in the car and were prepared to fight for the right to do so.

'Thanks for the lift, Mr Stewart,' she called back when they had all finally dismounted, then immediately she began walking the boys away towards the magnificent gates.

An amused look in his shrewd gold-flecked hazel eyes, Iain watched for a moment, then drove off.

'They won't open,' one of the boys exclaimed, pushing hard and peering through the gates and along the drive. 'We don't live here, Mummy, did you forgot?'

'Forget,' Mary corrected him automatically. 'No, I didn't.' She hustled him away back to the road. 'Mr Stewart just presumed we lived there.'

'What's "pesume"?' Making a super-human effort, the young boy managed to whistle a sound something like the word, his twin joining in and trying to out-rival him.

'Well, it means not really knowing but just guessing instead,' Mary said, which confused the boys still further so they contented themselves with holding her hands and skipping back with her around the corner to a little side road where they mounted some worn and broken cement steps leading up to a rather dilapidated second-floor flat.

The phone was ringing as they pushed open the front door. It was Andrew.

'I've had an idea,' he started by saying. 'I'm needing a temporary job and you need temporary help. What better than that we should help one another?'

'Are you crazy? What sort of job could I give you?' asked Mary.

'Child-minder. You said your present one wants to go to see her family in South Africa; well, let her go now until August first and I'll take over meanwhile. I need to make a living until I can start in orthopaedics.'

'Well, look, we can't discuss this over the phone. Come round on Saturday for tea; it'll give me time between now and then to digest your offer. How much would you want for doing the job? That's a crucial point.'

'Um, yes—I've been busy with my calculator trying to figure out how much I'd need in order to survive.'

'*If* you survive,' Mary stressed. 'My twins aren't exactly angels!'

'No, well, I had younger brothers and sisters so am well qualified to cope with anything your offspring can try on.'

'Then give me an idea of what you would cost me.'

'Food, accommodation and five pounds a week pocket money. How's that for an offer you can't refuse?'

'I'll give it a good think, and I must consult Debbie-Ann first. Anyway, come on Saturday; the kids are clamouring for their tea right now. I'll need to get Debbie-Ann's approval and her opinion of you. . .she's the sane, sensible type, wise for her years—besides, she's very fond of my boys, wouldn't want you to spoil all the good work she's done on them already. Also we'll have to know we can trust you.'

'Two selection boards approved of me.'

'So you said.'

'And I was given the orthopaedic appointment.'

'Just so. But how do I know you wouldn't want to try out your surgery skills on my sons?'

'Or on you?'

'You don't aim to be a plastic surgeon, do you?'

'Unnecessary in your case,' Andrew said flatteringly.

'No soft-soaping!' insisted Mary. 'Come anyway. We'll size you up character-wise. There are questions to be asked. I don't really know anything about you.'

'Nor do I know anything about you or your family. Your sons might terrorise me!'

'If you're not as firm as Debbie-Ann is with them, they might.'

'And you might harbour a tyrant under that sweet attractive exterior of yours?'

'Come and find out. This phone call must be costing you a fortune and I thought you were the poorest of the poor?'

'This is the sprat that catches the mackerel,' he began, quoting, but Mary was already putting down the phone. Within seconds however, it rang again.

'You didn't tell me your address,' Andrew complained, so Mary gave it. 'You'll find us easily,' she added, her mischievous streak coming to the fore again. 'Look for a large country mansion standing in its own grounds behind huge ornate gates. Come at four.'

'Saturday? You did say Saturday?'

'I did.'

'Well, I might be a bit late because I'll have to walk.'

'Then try limping a bit and watch out for Mr Stewart. He offers lifts to people who limp.'

Mary put down the phone in order to rescue a tin of baked beans from the boys, each claiming the right to open it.

'Neither of you until you're twelve,' she insisted, which kept them busy trying to work out how many years there were between three and a half and twelve.

Saturday came bringing with it a very exhausted Andrew, who declared he had had to walk miles looking for a country mansion bearing their address.

'Oh, please forgive me,' Mary said abjectly. 'I must have let my stupid sense of humour get the better of me again. Anyhow, it was a good practice for your initiative and you'll need plenty of that when dealing with my twins. All the same, I'm sorry I misled you. I really will have to take myself in hand.' Even as she spoke, she was disentangling her sons from life-threatening wrestling holds they had learnt at playschool.

'They're certainly real boys, aren't they?' Andrew

separated them just as they were about to strangle one another. . . 'How can you tell which is which?'

'By counting their freckles,' Mary said unhelpfully. 'Rob has a few more than Richie. . .or is it the other way round?' She scratched her head, frustrated and confused.

'It's the other way round,' said Debbie-Ann, bursting into the little lounge with a tray of tea and cookies.

A cookie in hand, 'Can you play football?' one of the twins asked Andrew.

'And cwicket?' added the other.

'Better than you can, I'll bet,' Andrew grinned. 'I've had more time to practise.'

'C'puter games?' the boys asked eagerly, in unison.

'I invent them.'

They sidled towards him. 'We haven't got a c'puter,' they moaned plaintively, their blue eyes mournful. . .

Andrew gave a sigh of relief and winked at Debbie-Ann. 'That lets me off the hook!' he murmured, adding, to Mary, 'This is getting to be worse than that interview the other day!'

'I'll bath the twins and put them to bed,' offered Debbie-Ann, 'then we can talk without fear of interruption.'

'One of my odd jobs in Australia was to look after seven little ones,' Andrew told Mary as they started clearing up the dirty dishes.

'Seven?' She eyed him disbelievingly. 'What help did you have?'

'None, there was only me.'

'What ages were they?'

'All the same age, six weeks old.'

'And all belonging to the same parents?' Mary picked up a cup and washed it. 'You're having me on, aren't you?'

He took the cup from her, to dry it. 'No, I'm not.'

'Then you shouldn't have been allowed to look after the babies, not without special training.'

'Oh, they weren't babies,' Andrew replied casually. 'they were kittens!'

So Mary chuckled, grabbed another tea-towel and threw it at him. Just then Debbie-Ann walked back in. She was looking thoughtful.

'Do you really think you could look after Rob and Richie?' she asked Andrew, her normally smooth brow puckered in serious thought. 'They're not exactly the world's easiest duo.'

'I could see that for myself,' he replied, equally in earnest. 'Nevertheless, I'm sure I can handle them. I couldn't cook like this, though.' He munched another cookie.

'Neither could I,' Debbie-Ann said with her usual frankness. 'That's why I bought them from the homemade cakes shop around the corner!'

They laughed together and, looking from one to the other of them, Mary sensed a possible beginning of a romance. But although she smiled, her heart ached. Romance, she reflected sadly, was already over in her own case.

CHAPTER TWO

ON DUTY for the weekend, Mary returned to work in her usual accident and emergency department the next morning looking for an opportunity to mention to her consultant that she had been given the staff-grade job at the Royal Glen Hospital.

She was sure he would be pleased for her sake, being fully aware of the problems she might have to face in the future, especially perhaps as her twins grew older.

However, Mr Drew was not available just then, and the doctor who had been on all night wanted to hand over to Mary the patients who were still in X-Ray, but also to make sure she would have some pre-knowledge of their various injuries and illnesses to help her in her review of their X-rays upon their return to Casualty.

Looking at the exhausted, sleep-deprived SHO, Mary concentrated on what he was saying so that he could feel free to go to bed confident that he had left his patients in capable and knowledgeable hands.

She remembered only too vividly all the many occasions she had felt just as desperate for sleep after equally long hours on duty through busy nights, so understandingly she packed him off to bed with an assurance that she had taken in all the information he had passed on, then, after a

brief chat to some of the nurses, she took the first
card from the doctors' box.

Reading what the triage nurse had written
regarding the patient, she went to the waiting area
and called for the person named on the card to
come to her.

A man described as a builder hobbled along.
'Dropped a paving stone on my foot, I did,' he
explained, trying to look cheerful. So Mary exam-
ined his foot, found it beginning to swell, had him
supplied with crutches and sent him along to get
an X-ray taken.

'You don't live far from the hospital, do you?'
she said to him when he returned and the nurses
had fitted a double tubigrip over the injured foot.
'Did someone come with you?'

'Yes.' He nodded. 'A younger sister. She's in
the waiting area.'

So Mary went along armed with the sister's
name and read it out. There was no response
from anyone. She called the name again, looking
directly towards the only young woman sitting
there. Finally she managed to catch her eye and
beckoned to her, only to have her spring to her
feet, looking scared stiff.

'You don't want me,' the young woman
declared, panicking a little. 'I'm not a patient!'

Mary smiled placatingly. 'Don't worry, I know
that, but perhaps you would help your brother
along. . .we've given him crutches, but what he'll
need when he gets home is to have ice packed
around his ankle to reduce the swelling. Frozen
peas might do the trick if you haven't any ice.'

Looking at Mary suspiciously as if the idea of using frozen peas was nothing but a bad joke, the young woman hastily helped her brother away from Casualty. Glad to leave it, Mary suspected.

'The brother knows about using frozen peas,' she murmured to the nurse with her, 'so he'll be all right even if the sister doubts my word.' She paused. 'Oh listen, what's this?'

A small boy was coming in screaming that he'd been bitten by a 'wild' hamster. He seemed to want the world to know he was suffering.

'The poor darling,' sympathised his mother, an arm around him. 'It really was a savage bite; one can't blame him for screaming.' However, he screamed even louder when given a tetanus toxoid injection, staring at Mary afterwards with accusing, baleful eyes.

'He should have been given one of these injections ages ago,' Mary murmured to the nurse after the mother had taken the unrestrainable boy away. 'All children should be protected against tetanus from the word go, then the injection wouldn't come as such a shock.'

It came as quite a relief to have a very pleasant man take over from the spoilt little boy. 'My granddaughter had been playing with her dog, trying to retrieve her slipper from him in a lively tug of war, when I went to her aid, to protect her, and the dog nipped me instead!' he said with a wry but humorous grimace. 'Fortunately I've always kept topped up with tetanus jabs.'

'I'm glad someone has some sense,' Mary smiled, her annoyance soothed. 'I don't think you'll have any further trouble with the bite,' she said, after examining it, and left the nurses to take over the treatment of it while she tended a rugger player who had had his jaw broken in a head-on collision with another player during a practice match.

'One can tell there's a break in the jaw because of the irregularity of his teeth, and the tenderness in front of his ear,' Mary said, instructing the more inexperienced SHOs, those who had not long finished their year as housemen whereas Mary had already served over a year as an A and E SHO, and was well equipped to train others to become casualty officers.

'Now we test for sensation along the line of teeth,' she continued, 'and see, there's a tooth missing. It must have been swallowed or inhaled. Ask the patient if he had had to cough,' she suggested, and upon the reply that he had, but had thought it due to swallowing blood, 'listen to his chest,' Mary instructed next. 'There's reduced air entry into one area of it, so send him for a chest X-ray, also for an OPG—an X-ray of his jaw.

'You'll find an OPG a bit eerie but interesting,' she told the patient, 'they'll give you a lollypop stick to bite on, well, it's a spatula really, and they'll put your head in a dome-like thing with an opening at the back. A fitted camera moves along taking a continuous film of the jaw.'

Studying the X-ray afterwards, Mary pointed out to the SHOs that the mandible was broken in two places, and that the tooth was lodged in one of the bronchi of his left lung, so the patient

needed to be referred to both the facial maxillary
department and the thoracic surgeon.

This done, 'Now we can safely leave him to
their expert care,' she said, leading the way back
to the doctors' box so that they could make necessary inroads into the lengthening list of new
patients, those who had had to be kept waiting
while the injured rugby player had needed so
much attention, and while the necessary teaching
had had to be given for the sake of future patients
who might suffer similar injuries.

Then, with the waiting time cut down to an
acceptable level, Mary again sought out Mr Drew
to tell him she would be taking up the new staff
doctor appointment at the Royal Glen in one
month's time.

'I'll be sorry to lose you,' he said, 'you'll be
sadly missed here, but congratulations on the new
appointment, Mary. I can't think of anyone who
deserves it more.'

Although she said little, her smile showed her
gratitude, for she was sure his written reference
must have helped enormously in getting her selected for the job she needed so badly. A job which,
as she reminded herself when inclined to regret
having to leave the Nightingale Hospital, would
leave her with so much more free time to spend
with her boys, would rarely if ever take her away
from them at night, and would more than make
up for the earlier days when she was working
sometimes for over one hundred and thirty hours
a week and felt permanently exhausted.

Nevertheless, 'I shall be sorry to leave here,'

she found herself saying quite sincerely to Mr Drew. 'It's a happy environment, everyone so friendly.' She paused, thinking of Iain Stewart and doubting whether she would find the same friendliness in his department, instead foreseeing all sorts of difficulties arising when trying to work with him. Was he, she wondered, going to prove to be her stumbling block and ruin everything?'

'Yes, this place certainly gives the lie to those media portrayals of casualty departments,' Mr Drew was saying. 'Most of them must leave viewers with the impression that our staff are forever either arguing or having affairs! It's a great pity the general public is being deluded to such an extent.' And, tut-tutting woefully, he went back to his office while Mary helped herself to yet another card from the doctors' box.

Just what would Iain Stewart be like to work with? she was asking herself again, wondering how she was going to get him to accept her in her new role. For a start, she decided, she would always wear the badge stating her new status, and never, if she could help it, wear a white coat. That should help him identify her as different, if nothing else! Also she would work only the hours she was contracted to work, unless there was a real emergency, and even then she would make sure she took off other hours in lieu of the extras she worked.

It wasn't that she was work-shy, her consultant could verify that; no, it was simply that she had Rob and Richie to consider and in no way was she going to neglect them, not even if it meant

having daily battles with the obviously intractable
Iain Stewart!

Thinking the way she was, it came as quite a
shock to see him in her canteen when she went
along there to have some lunch. He was sharing
a table with Mr Drew.

The canteen was crowded. Suddenly overcome
by shyness, she started to retreat, but Mr Drew,
seeing her, beckoned to show her there was an
empty chair beside him. Rather than risk appearing to arrogantly ignore his invitation, she had no
recourse but to walk over to the table.

He started to introduce her to Iain who, however, interrupted to say a short, 'We have met.'

'Oh,' said the consultant, slightly taken aback.
'So you know each other? Iain and I belong to
the same golf club, Mary. Do you play golf?'

'Only the miniature variety,' she said, colouring
up because Iain seemed to be eyeing her so
slightingly.

'But then you have quite a handicap, haven't
you?' he muttered, and she was sure he was being
derogatory about her twins.

Mr Drew laughed a little uneasily as if sensing
the discord between Iain and Mary, then he
pushed his empty plate aside and rose to his feet.
'Look at that time!' he exclaimed, staring up at
the clock on the wall. 'And I've a conference to
attend. No golfing this afternoon,' he said to Iain.
'Saturday at eleven perhaps?'

'I'll try and make it,' said Iain, then rose as if
to follow him, except that he halted behind Mary's
chair and, 'Enjoy your lunch,' he said in a low

murmur, his hand brushing against her neck when giving her a light pat on the shoulder. Surprised into catching her breath, she jerked backwards and it seemed as if her head would have impulsively rested against his chest had he not hurried off to catch up with Mr Drew to begin chatting to him without as much as a backward glance towards Mary left sitting alone at the table.

Now what did he have to touch me for? she asked herself angrily, hoping he had not read more into her surprised reaction than that it was an impulsive and natural response to being taken off-guard, and nothing more than that. . .

Deciding she no longer felt like having a meal, she left the canteen and returned to Casualty.

'You weren't at lunch for long,' remarked Staff Nurse Gabrielle, a close friend, as they went along to the canteen for a tea-break later in the afternoon, 'and you came back looking peaky. Why?'

'I suddenly lost my appetite,' Mary said woefully, without further explanation until a moment or two later when she added, 'Besides, I wanted to make sure the two dog-bitten patients had been put on short antibiotic courses.'

'You wouldn't have forgotten to see to that,' Gabrielle reassured her. 'Anyway, not to worry, everything's in order: the courses of antibiotics, complete with full directions, were safely handed over.'

'Oh, good, I couldn't be sure; I seem to be all at sixes and sevens these days.'

'It's getting the promotion, that's what's done

it, gone to your head!' Gabrielle smiled then saddened. 'I'm glad you've got the staff job but I'll
certainly miss you here. D'you think I could get
a transfer to the Royal Glen?'

'I wish you would, but if you can't, at least you
could pop into my flat whenever you're free.'

'You mightn't be there!'

'Well, Andrew might be; he'd entertain you
until I arrived back.'

'Andrew? Who's he?'

'My temporary child-minder.'

'A male child-minder?'

Mary grinned, 'And a doctor, no less!'

'Wow! That's a turn-up for the books!'

'It's a perfectly harmless arrangement,' Mary
said chidingly. 'Debbie-Ann is going to visit her
parents in Cape Town and Andrew has nowhere
to live until he takes over his new job as registrar
locum at the Glen on August the first, so he's
obliging me by looking after the twins in return
for accommodation, food and a fiver a week. I
met him at the interviews. He seems a thoroughly
nice person and the boys will be well looked after,
besides having fun with him. Debbie-Ann
approves of him and you know how protective
she is over the twins; she wouldn't leave them
unless she was sure they'd be in good hands;
neither would I, not even for a minute.'

'I know you wouldn't,' said Gabrielle. 'When
can I meet him?'

'I warn you, I think he has already fallen for
Debbie-Ann.'

'Still, while the cat's away the mouse can play,'

Gabrielle winked meaningly. 'How long will she be gone for?'

'You're a hopeless flirt,' Mary denounced her laughingly. 'It sounds to me as if Andrew is in danger of being torn to pieces between you and Debbie-Ann!'

'You haven't fallen for him yourself by any chance, have you? Oh, no, you'd rather have the admirable Iain laying siege to your heart, wouldn't you!' Gabrielle teased, to immediately look aghast as she obviously realised the effect her words could have on one as sensitive as Mary, whose deep-seated sense of loss over the premature death of her husband was so great that, as Gabrielle knew only too well, she dared not allow herself to grieve, instead putting up a brave front always, for the sake of her sons. Gabrielle sickened, looking furious with herself for possibly adding to Mary's struggles against her unhappiness and difficulties.

But just then, in time to save the day as far as Gabrielle was concerned, Mary's bleep went off, alerting her to the drama of an emergency. Without waiting to say or hear another word, she raced back to Casualty.

'A motorist skidded on oil already spilt on the motorway during a previous accident, hit the central barrier, is trapped in his car, firemen trying to cut him out,' Mr Drew briefed her hurriedly. 'Get ready, we're going with the Flying Squad.'

'Me? Why me?' Mary's eyes brightened. Usually one of the even more experienced doctors accompanied Mr Drew on such emergency call-outs.

'Because when you start your staff-grade job you'll be one of the senior doctors so you need experience in this sort of thing,' Mr Drew pointed out.

Mary smiled her gratitude and speedily collected the necessary fluorescent trousers and jacket from the major accident store-room and, carrying them, plus a hard safety-type hat labelled 'Doctor', went back to await the arrival of the Flying Squad ambulance.

Mr Drew smiled at her. 'How's your adrenalin flowing?' he asked. 'One never knows what one will have to face up to in cases like this where there could well be multiple injuries, other motorists being involved.'

Then he suddenly laughed outright, unable to help himself as Mary struggled to walk wearing a pair of oversized trousers, her skirt tucked into the wide waistband, her feet encased in large and scruffy, once white wellingtons.

'Here, take these.' He handed her the fluorescent trousers he was holding ready to put on over his suit trousers. 'My portly figure can do with the extra width of those you have,' he said, sobering up, 'while these look rather too small for me!'

The jacket also was much too big for Mary's slender figure, but, the ambulance arriving just then, she made do with it, having no alternative really, the teeming rain calling for everyone to wear as much protective clothing as possible.

Heavy clouds brought dusk forward, and everything looked unusually threatening. An air of foreboding kept everyone tense at first although no one allowed jangling nerves to show, the whole emergency team of two doctors, an experienced nurse and the ambulance crew of technician and paramedic forcing themselves to keep on the alert ready to give whatever help would be needed.

'Can you get through to ambulance control and find out how many people have been injured?' Mr Drew asked the paramedic driving Eagle One, the Flying Squad ambulance.

But by the time an answer could be received, the scene of the accident had been reached and the emergency team found out that there was just the trapped man for them to see to; the other less seriously injured victims had already been taken to hospital.

The trapped motorist, in a semi-conscious state, was lolling awkwardly back in the driver's seat, a paramedic fitting him with a hard cervical collar. Becoming aware that the hospital trauma team had arrived, the paramedic turned.

'I'm glad you're here,' he said; 'this chap's blood-pressure is OK but he's losing quite a lot of blood, is in pain too, but I haven't been able to get a line in.'

Mary, ignoring the broken glass and very uncomfortable with water dripping down her neck, nevertheless tried hard but found it quite impossible to reach the motorist's uninjured arm.

'Hold on a sec, Doc,' called a cheery voice behind her. 'If we remove the passenger door for you, will that be of help?' And straight away the fireman dealt with the door, enabling Mary to slide on to the passenger seat beside the patient and insert the necessary lines into his veins.

Ignoring the heavy downpour, rain falling as straight as rods through the car's buckled and broken roof, the nurse handed over the prepared vials of analgesia and the intravenous fluids which Mary then gave to the patient.

Mr Drew suggesting a spinal board should be used, the ambulance crew brought one over and carefully strapped the injured man on to it. The firemen were then able to at last release him from the car.

With Mr Drew supervising the placing of the accident victim on to the floating stretcher, and his connection to the monitoring equipment in Eagle One, the whole emergency team accompanied the patient to the hospital.

'Could you radio through, via Ambulance Control, to tell our department how long we'll be and that we'll need the resuscitation room prepared?' Mary asked the ambulance crew politely but authoritatively, surprised to find herself so capable of taking charge, allowing the already exhausted Mr Drew to rest back a little, much to his relief.

She studied the patient again. 'His facial injuries are very bad,' she muttered to Mr Drew. 'I wish he'd had one of those airbags now being fitted in cars to prevent drivers hitting the steering-wheel when they crash. Just think of the suffering he would have been saved. Every car should have one!'

Nodding agreement, Mr Drew watched her eyes filling with pity as she listened to the man's moans. But, suddenly realising what was implied by the very fact that he could moan, she cheered up, encouraged.

'Listen,' she exclaimed aloud, 'his conscious level is improving!'

Greatly relieved, and inwardly giving thanks for the rising hope of a successful result to her first experience with the Flying Squad, Mary smiled at Mr Drew. A very watery smile, but a smile nevertheless.

CHAPTER THREE

THE next piece of news coming through from Ambulance Control was a little unnerving for Mary, however. There were no more empty beds available in her own hospital, all having been taken up by the injured persons who had been brought in earlier on from the scene of the accident.

'Anyway, the regional neuro-surgical unit in the Royal Glen is the best place for our patient,' Mr Drew said, and Mary agreed with him, although cringing a little because she knew she would have to face Iain Stewart again and, dressed as she was, she would have preferred to hide away from him. He would be sure to be scathing, she told herself, wondering how she could avoid him.

As it happened, however, he was there waiting to receive the new patient and, while having him taken into the resuscitation-room, Mr Drew supervising the transfer on to a trolley, Mary, steeling herself, accompanied Iain to give him a clear history of what had happened, including precise information regarding the head injury, facial injury and compound fracture of the right arm and left lower leg, and vetted her concern about the young man's neck and back.

'Also I suspect a pelvis injury,' she added, 'and I've taken a sample of blood for cross-matching.'

She handed the small phial to one of the casualty officers to be labelled and sent off to the laboratory.

Iain looked quite impressed, but then he noticed what she was wearing, and for the next few moments seemed preoccupied in trying to prevent his face showing amusement.

'It's a bit hot in here,' he managed to say at last, although his voice still sounded rather strangled as he added, 'I should shed your outer garments if I were you!' Then, turning away from Mary with something like relief, he reviewed the new patient's X-rays—which had just been completed—then arranged for a computerised tomography scan of the injured man's brain.

'Come with me to watch the scan being done,' he suggested to Mary when, with his help, she had finally managed to discard the ill-fitting jacket and over-trousers, and, because Mr Drew had already left on Eagle One to return to the Nightingale Hospital, she stayed behind, a double purpose in mind, wanting not only to see the scan unit working, but also thinking it a good opportunity to familiarise herself with the resuscitation room of what was to be her future department.

Meanwhile, after the scan, the patient went into Intensive Care to stay there until the orthopaedic surgeons took him to Theatre, and, left alone with Mary for a few seconds, Iain surprised her with an appreciative, 'You did a good job with the roadside resuscitation.'

The compliment so surprised her that she blushed, and when he followed his words with an

offer to drive her back to her hospital to return the
borrowed clothes to the Nightingale's major accident store-room, and to collect her handbag from
her locker, then drive her home, she completely
forgot she had misled him into thinking she lived
in the mansion up the drive behind the ornate gates.

So she was thoroughly caught out and nonplussed as to what to reply, when, having taken
the fluorescent trousers, jacket and safety helmet
back to her hospital, she returned to the car and
after driving her on to the big ornamental gates,
Iain turned to her, tipped her chin up towards
him so that she was forced to meet his eyes,
and said, 'You don't live here, do you? Be
honest, now.'

As she told Debbie-Ann afterwards, she could
not have felt worse had she been a schoolgirl seen
to be playing truant!

'I suppose I'll have to confess,' she had murmured in a very small voice. 'You'll have to
reverse to the little side street we just passed. I
have a second-floor flat there, nothing as splendid
as this place I'm afraid.'

Iain made no comment, he simply followed her
directions and drew up beside the worn steps.

'Will the boys be asleep?' he asked then.

'I doubt it.'

'And you don't want to invite me in?'

'I'd rather not, if you don't mind. The place
will be in a terrible mess. We can't tidy up until
the boys have settled down for the night, and it's
probably bath-time now.'

'We?' Iain repeated.

'I have a child-minder.' Mary moved to get out of the car. 'Now, if you'll excuse me, I'd better go in and give a hand.'

'Of course.' Iain reached over and opened the door for her. 'Next time I see you with your twins, perhaps you'd introduce me?'

'See one and you've seen them both,' Mary brightened, thinking of them. 'They're as alike as. . .'

'Peas in a pod?'

She actually laughed. 'For want of a better simile, yes!'

He stood out on the pavement with her, appearing loath to go, so she ran up the steps, called, 'Thanks for the lift,' and disappeared into the shabby porch at the entrance to the second-floor flat.

After a few seemingly reflective moments, Iain climbed back into his car and drove away. Had he been able to look back he might have seen the front curtain move. Mary had not been able to resist taking another peep at him, she was so bemused by the apparent change in his attitude towards her.

So, he could be nice, could he? She smiled to herself, letting the curtain fall back into place. But what must he think of her and the way she had tried to mislead him? She would have to be more careful in future, for obviously he was not a man who could be easily fooled.

Quickly changing out of her remaining grubby and still partly blood-stained clothing, she donned a heather-blue sweater and black leggings and went along to help Debbie-Ann get the twins out of the bath, much to their joint disapproval. Water was everywhere!

'We'll get complaints from the downstairs flat at this rate,' Mary muttered, grabbing one of her sons before there was time even to say 'hello', then, while explaining to Debbie-Ann about the accident keeping her so late in getting home, and the embarrassing drive with Iain, she handed her one of the few dry towels left and, together towelling away at the boys, they finally got them into their pyjamas and sitting at the kitchen's small work-surface drinking cocoa and eating bread and honey.

Then came the routine brushing of teeth, night prayers and bedtime cuddles. Finally, stealing out of their room, wishing to give the impression to the boys that they were expected to be already asleep, Mary switched off the light and took a deep breath, hoping her ruse would have had some success, although pretty sure there was little chance it would succeed.

'Listen to them,' she sighed to Debbie-Ann, 'they're pillow-fighting already!'

'What they need is a man to discipline them before it's too late,' Debbie-Ann muttered. 'Andrew what'sisname might do the trick.'

Mary was already preparing a late tea, poached eggs on toast. 'I doubt it.' She shook her head. 'If you ask me, he's even worse than they are!' But she spoke with a smile, as if enjoying the thought of him.

'Where will he sleep?' Debbie-Ann asked.

'I don't know. There might be a room going vacant in this building; I'll have to ask. A sort of bedsitter. But I did offer accommodation as part of the package.'

'What about my room? He could have that while I'm away.'

'You wouldn't mind?'

'Not at all, as long as he isn't going to take it over permanently.' Debbie-Ann gave Mary a surprising look of apprehension, almost as if she feared Andrew might become more to Mary than just a child-minder. 'After all, we hardly know him,' she added lamely.

'However, you do know *me*,' Mary admonished her. 'And you know Andrew enough to have fallen a little in love with him already.'

Debbie pulled a wry face, 'That's the trouble,' she said frankly. 'I wouldn't like him to fall for anyone else while I'm away and so ruin my chances when I come back!'

'Don't worry.' Mary poured the freshly brewed tea and put plates to warm for the eggs and toast. 'I'll keep him safe for you!'

Debbie, already colouring up, looked a little ashamed of herself. 'I'm talking nonsense,' she said by way of excuse. 'What must you be thinking of me?'

'I think you're one of the nicest, most human people I know,' Mary smiled, 'and I very much hope Andrew thinks the same. But don't stay away too long; Gabrielle seems to fancy him too!'

'Thanks for the warning. Don't invite her here until I come back, will you?'

'Too late, she knows she's welcome any time; she's the best friend I have in the hospital.'

'Then keep her there,' begged Debbie, 'help them to avoid one another. It should be easy, especially as Andrew won't be starting to work in the Royal Glen Hospital until August.'

'You're serious, aren't you?' Mary looked surprised. 'And you're forgetting that Gabrielle doesn't work in the Royal Glen, so he isn't likely to come across her at all.'

'Unless she comes here. You say you've already given her the "open sesame" for whenever she wants to come.'

'Oh Debbie, you don't blame me for making her welcome, do you? She always has been, and——' Mary sounded quite distressed '—always will be. I don't turn my back on my friends, you know that, and Gabrielle has been a great help to me, just as you have. I'm very fond of you both and would hate to do anything to hurt either of you.'

Debbie-Ann stood silent.

'I'm hating myself!' Mary said suddenly, her meal left lying cold before her. 'Here we are, having our first confrontation ever, and all because of Andrew. Honestly, I'm beginning to wish I had never met him! You're upset, I'm upset, and Gabrielle is likely to be just as sick about it all. I never thought we would have this sort of trouble; we've got on so well together until now.'

She blinked away an unbidden tear.

The next minute Debbie-Ann was beside her, an

arm about her shoulders. 'It's all my fault,' she was saying, 'I'm being stupid. I think I'm just scared. Scared about my father's illness, scared I'll be losing my close contact with your twins, scared our friendship won't survive the enforced break. . .'

'And scared you'll lose Andrew to Gabrielle while you're away?' Mary smiled mistily, looking back at Debbie-Ann. 'You mustn't worry about that. If he's to be the man for you, he will be. A month is nothing compared with the lifetime you have before you; in fact, it could well be that he will find out what life is like without you around, and long for your return. Anything could happen!'

'Of course.' Debbie-Ann smiled too and, going back to her place at the table, sat down again, but before she could find out that the egg on toast and tea had grown unappetisingly cold, there was a ring on the front doorbell.

'It might be Andrew,' eagerly she jumped to her feet, 'I'll open the door to him!'

But, to the surprise of both girls, it was Iain.

Mary sat stock still, listening to his voice. What had she done wrong? she wondered, going over the afternoon's accident procedure in her mind. Then Debbie-Ann returned from the little porch.

'It's the casualty consultant from the Royal Glen Hospital,' she murmured quietly. 'He says you left your boots in his car.'

'Boots?' Mary looked bemused for a moment. 'Oh, my RTA boots! I remember now, he put them in the boot of his car because they were so muddy and wet. Show him into the lounge, Debbie. . .'

She was already hastily tidying herself up in front of the mottled wall mirror which hung suspended over a tiny old-fashioned bedroom-type iron mantelpiece.

'Your hair looks as if it hasn't seen a comb in a week of Sundays!' Debbie whispered.

'Who cares? He's seen me looking worse than this! Besides, I'm not out to impress!' Mary playfully half pushed Debbie-Ann out of the kitchen.

'Then why are you titivating yourself?' Debbie-Ann grinned, teasing and making a quick exit.

'Habit, pure habit,' was all Mary had time to retort before Iain seemed to meet Debbie-Ann in a head-on clash in the tiny porch. Apologising to each other, they entered the little lounge, Mary close on their heels.

'I've left the boots in the car,' said Iain. 'Thought you'd like to drop them off at your hospital yourself.'

'Well, I don't particularly want them in here,' Mary replied; 'we've quite enough clutter as it is. Will you be passing the hospital?'

'Yes.' He frowned, however, and hesitated. 'But I wouldn't know where to find the Nightingale's A and E clothing store, and I take it that's where they came from? Could you come and return them yourself?'

Mary sighed. 'I suppose it's up to me to do so.'

'Your boys are asleep?'

'I daren't look!'

'I'll be here,' Debbie-Ann reminded her. 'Don't worry about them.'

'Oh, I haven't introduced you. . .Debbie-Ann de Villiers, meet Mr Iain Stewart.'

The two shook hands.

'Debbie-Ann is my friend and wonder helper,' Mary said, looking towards her with an appreciative smile. 'I honestly don't know what I would do without her, or what my twins would get up to were she not here to control them.'

'She'd manage,' Debbie-Ann asserted, nodding to Iain. 'She always does.'

'Well, let's get rid of the boots,' Iain suggested. 'They might be needed for some other accident tonight or tomorrow.'

'Oh, no, I hope not,' Mary saddened, thinking of the badly hurt patient. 'How is the young man we brought in?' she asked Iain.

'In Intensive Care, but we're hopeful,' he said, leading the way back to the little porch.

'I won't be long, Debbie-Ann,' promised Mary. 'You don't mind if I go along, do you?'

'Of course not.' Debbie-Ann smiled. 'We'll make a fresh meal when you return.'

'Did I interrupt one you were having?' Iain asked as he walked down the outside steps with Mary.

'It had already been interrupted,' she answered, shrugging nonchalantly, then said nothing more until after she had deposited the boots back into the major accident store-room of her hospital and rejoined Iain in his car.

Waiting until she had adjusted her seat-belt, he suggested he should treat her to a meal before taking her back to the flat.

'Why?' she asked in her customary guarded way.

'To make up for the meal I made you miss.'

'You didn't make me miss it. It was cold and unpalatable minutes before you came.'

'Really? Then you must be as hungry as I am. I've had nothing since lunch—if one could call a meagre portion of canteen shepherd's pie and a few cold mushy peas a lunch. Dine with me in my favourite restaurant. I hate dining alone.'

'You usually have company?' Mary enquired, interested. She glanced up at him. His profile had softened, unexpected humour playing around his lips once again.

'What would you expect of a single man?' he asked.

Then his voice and face sobered. 'Mr Drew was telling me about your husband losing his life when caught in an ambush while delivering food to starving refugees a few years ago. You must be very proud of him for the work he was trying to do,' he said softly.

'I am.' Mary was unable to disguise the gulp in her throat, the tear in her voice.

'Did he live to see the twins?' Iain spoke in a caring tone without glancing at her, instead concentrating on the winding road ahead.

'No. He knew I was expecting our first child and was very happy about that.' Mary's answer came muffled, but try as she would she was unable to stop confiding in Iain, he appeared so mature and genuinely sympathetic, and it seemed an age since she had been able to give vent to her grief

to anyone. Always before it had necessary for her
to hide her true feelings.

'He didn't know we were having twins,' she
continued, looking away. 'I didn't get the chance
to tell him. He would have been as delighted as
I was, although I didn't know myself until just a
month before they were born.'

'What are their names?'

Still appreciating his interest, 'Rob and Richie,'
she told him. Then, peering ahead through the
windscreen, 'Where are we?' she asked apprehen-
sively, suddenly realising that, wherever they were,
mountains instead of buildings were silhouetting
themselves against the sky at either side, soaring up
into bright moonlight and a clear sky.

'I've been talking too much.' She spoke regret-
fully. 'I should have gone straight back to the flat,
Debbie-Ann will be getting anxious.'

'I'm taking you to my favourite haunt where
meals are superb and the service excellent. You
can phone your child-minder from there.'

'You might have asked before driving me so
far out of the city,' Mary demurred. 'I had no
idea we had travelled so far.'

'I knew exactly what I was doing,' Iain stated.
'So just relax and trust me. . .look, here we are.'

He parked the car in the foreground of a
delightful Scottish castle and led her up the wide
fountain-edged steps into what must once have
been a baronial hall. There he was immediately
greeted with enthusiasm, being obviously well
known to the staff.

It had been a long time since Mary had dined

in such elegant surroundings. She drew back. 'I
can't go in there,' she protested when Iain tried
to lead her to the table where the restaurant manager was holding back a chair in readiness for her.
'I haven't even had a chance to tidy myself up!'
she complained. 'Debbie-Ann said my hair looked
as if it hadn't seen a comb for a month of Sundays
and her blunt criticisms usually have far more than
a grain of truth to give them substance!'

'Look, stay here by the public telephones, ring
your Debbie-Ann then slip into the adjacent
powder room and straighten yourself up. I'll keep
the manager occupied. . .he won't even notice
you, I promise.'

'I didn't know whether to be flattered or
insulted by that remark,' Mary told Debbie-Ann
over the phone. 'I wish I could come home. I feel
trapped!'

'Take advantage of the situation and have a good
meal, then come,' Debbie-Ann suggested. 'The boys
are sound asleep at last,' she added, then—sounding rather self-conscious, 'Andrew has just walked
in,' she murmured, 'so don't hurry yourself!'

Which left Mary feeling more trapped than
ever. Nevertheless she forced herself to sound
agreeable while ringing off, although well aware
that Debbie would not be too pleased to have her
interrupt a possible tête-à-tête with Andrew, so
was really urging her to stay out.

Attempting to smooth down her flyaway hair
and sweep it to one side in the hope that it might
add a little glamour to her weary, unmade-up
face, she joined Iain at the candlelit table.

CHAPTER FOUR

'I DON'T think it was fair of you to inveigle me here like this,' Mary burst out, seating herself opposite Iain. 'I'm very conscious of the fact that I am far from suitably dressed for such an occasion. Look at the other diners around. . .I feel like a poor relation!'

Iain raised his eyebrows but continued studying the menu.

'It's pretty obvious that you intended coming here all along, even had a table booked in advance,' she continued chastisingly.

He looked at her then. 'It did seem an opportunity for us to get to know one another better,' he replied seriously. 'Especially important now seeing that we're to work together in the future. A staff-grade doctor plays quite a significant part in the running of a department.'

Then suddenly his normally stern mouth softened, the likeness of a smile playing around his lips. 'Besides, I had to find an excuse to get you to myself. Douglas Drew warned me it might not be easy. Anyway, we're here now so what will you have to eat?'

He leaned towards her across the table. 'By the way,' he went on quietly, 'you might not consider your appearance appropriate for a place such as

this, but actually you look very nice, whatever it
is you're wearing.'

'You think I look better now than in the clothes
you saw me in after the RTA?' she asked win-
somely, then, as if her mind had again been taken
over by unhappy memories, a shadow crossed her
face, dulling the blue of her eyes.

Yet Iain appeared not to notice; instead he
replied in a humorous way, 'I claim the legal right
to remain silent in face of such a question!' then
once more asked her to decide what she wanted,
pointing out that the waiter was already approaching their table.

Reminded in some way of her meal with
Andrew, Mary—regaining her composure—felt
tempted to see what would happen if she suggested dry bread and water, but, uncertain as to
whether Iain's sense of humour would stretch that
far, she hesitated, looking at him as if wanting
him to make the menu decisions.

Which he did, albeit impatiently. 'We're in a
hurry, aren't we?' he reminded her. 'So what
about starting with smoked salmon followed by
Angus beef with oyster mushrooms and wild rice?'

'The same for both, sir?' The waiter seemed
relieved to have Iain nod decisively.

'We haven't time for all that,' Mary remonstrated, suggesting instead that they should miss
out on the starters.

Although obviously none too pleased at being
countermanded, nevertheless Iain ordered as
Mary wished, asking for only the second course.

'Wine, sir?' asked the wine waiter.

'No, I'll be driving. Just Highland mineral water for me,' Iain replied curtly, still out of humour because his plans were going awry.

'Iced water, please,' Mary requested, to the obvious further disappointment of the waiter.

'Wouldn't you prefer champagne?' Iain asked as the waiter walked away.

Mary shook her wavy fair hair into disarray again. 'I haven't had champagne since. . .' Her voice trailed away, her mind returning to her wedding-breakfast and the one or two celebration dinners she and Robert had enjoyed afterwards. He had not lived long enough to accumulate money for many such luxuries, she reflected.

Iain was watching her face almost as if he could read what she was thinking, her pain reflected in his own eyes, showing a genuine concern for her, had she but realised it. . .

'So you called your twins Rob and Richie,' he remarked as if to introduce happier thoughts, 'I take it your husband's name was Robert Richard?'

'I'd rather not talk about him just now, if you don't mind,' Mary replied, fearing that she was in danger of being disloyal to Robert's memory in some way by speaking of him while dining with Iain.

'I'm sorry,' Iain had the grace to say, 'I didn't mean to distress you.'

Mary was relieved to see the waiters approaching with their meal, and, given time to think, she realised she might have sounded very abrupt in her reply to Iain, so she tried to make up for it by chatting more freely as soon as the serving waiters had left them to themselves. . .

'Calling the twins Rob and Richie might sound corny,' she began; 'however, after the Caesarean operation and accompanying drugs, I wasn't capable of thinking straight, all I wanted was to have them named after Robert, with short, easy-to-remember names. Rob and Richie seemed to fit the bill somehow.'

That Iain disagreed she could tell from his quizzically raised eyebrows, so, embarrassed, she gabbled on a little breathlessly, 'You see, my husband had three Christian names, Robert Richard James, so my mother suggested that to provide the twins at least with different first initials so as not to confuse birth certificates and eventual school registers, et cetera, I should have one baptised Robert Angus and the other Jamie Richard, so I expect they'll be called Robert and Jamie when they go to school, don't you?'

Her voice almost died away. 'I just wanted to please Robert in my choice of names,' she explained shyly. 'He was nothing if not a true Scot.'

'With a surname like Macgregor, what else could one expect?' Iain remarked with a surprisingly understanding smile.

'My father insists on calling the boys Rob and Roy and I'm afraid I do too sometimes when they're nearly driving me up the wall! You're a Scot too, aren't you, so I expect you know all about Rob Roy?' Mary suggested, hoping Iain might help the awkward conversation along by finding something interesting to say.

However, he merely scratched his head pon-
deringly then, after a moment or two, muttered,
'Well, I know he was the outlaw whose violent
life was romanticised by Sir Walter Scott in his
novel *Rob Roy*,' he stated, then sat back in his
chair, studying his almost empty plate.

'If I remember correctly, that book was written
about a hundred years after Rob Roy turned to
banditry after losing his family fortunes.' Mary
pushed her still well-laden plate aside, less interested in eating than in proving to Iain that she
too knew some Scottish history.

'Only to get himself arrested and sentenced to
transportation—you know that too?' Iain raised
an eyebrow encouragingly.

'But pardoned in the end,' Mary said, smugly
correct, sure he was trying to amuse himself at
her expense by faulting her historical expertise.
'However, my twins might carry his name uninten-
tionally sometimes but I don't really want them
to emulate him!'

'With you as their mother, I'm sure they won't,'
Iain remarked, his unexpected instant gallantry
surprising Mary into rewarding him with a
gracious bow, achieving a mutual laugh.

'Some people might think they already are.'
She rushed the words to hide the embarrassing
realisation that she was finding Iain's company
surprisingly enjoyable.

But, 'Already are what?' he queried, puzzled.

'Copying Rob Roy.'

'Oh, I see what you mean. I'm sorry, my mind
was wandering. Is your hair really as soft and fine

as it looks?' He reached out a hand to touch it. 'Spun gold,' he declared it admiringly.

Mary's pale cheeks flushed pink. 'I thought we were supposed to be discussing the names of my twins?' she murmured.

'Yes, of course,' he agreed in an abstract way, slowly, as if unwillingly, withdrawing his hand. 'You were saying?' Then he frowned, looking down at her plate. 'You eat very slowly,' he remarked. 'I've almost finished, yet you've barely started. . .could it be that you drank too much iced water?'

'I seem to need a lot to help the food go down.' She looked awkward.

'But you feel all right? No real trouble with your digestion?' He seemed genuinely concerned.

Twisting around, Mary unhooked her handbag from the back of her chair. 'I can't wait for dessert or coffee,' she remarked, conscious of her increasingly painful inability to fully swallow even the small amount of food she had taken during the meal. Realising she was suffering an unnatural discomfort, she avoided answering Iain's question, not wishing to betray her growing anxiety about her condition, yet not knowing what to say without deepening his obvious suspicion that all was not as it should be with her. 'I'd like to go back to my flat right now if you don't mind.' Aware of the strange gurglings and hiccoughs besetting her and not wanting Iain to hear them, Mary pushed back her chair and stood up, surreptitiously pressing her folded arms across her middle in an effort to keep it quiet.

'Sit down again,' said Iain. 'Another few minutes won't hurt and here comes the coffee. I haven't ordered any dessert; you've had difficulty enough eating any of the main course.' His frown was both perplexed and anxious.

'Yes, I'm sorry about that,' Mary coloured up again, guiltily this time and perching uncomfortably on the edge of her chair. 'Nevertheless you provided a wonderful meal and I really have appreciated it even if I haven't been able to do it justice.' She started to fiddle with her bag and was obviously very ill at ease.

Iain sighed. 'I'd hoped that by the end of it we'd know each other a little better, but no such luck. You keep your inner self well hidden from me—I don't know why, but certainly I'm conscious of it all the time.'

Standing, in a lowered voice he muttered, 'I can't fathom you out, Mary, but I'll tell you this. . .just as still waters tempt one to disturb them to their very depths, you will only have yourself to blame if I find myself unable to resist a similar temptation.'

Then straightening, 'All right, let's go,' he said, abruptly. 'There were many questions I had planned to ask, but you don't invite questions. . . in fact you seem to deliberately avoid answering any.' His brow furrowed deeply. 'I'm none the wiser about you, and don't know where I stand at all, which I must say displeases rather than intrigues me. Being so on guard against each other won't make working together any easier.'

He reached out a hand to help her from her

chair but she managed by herself. 'I'm sorry,' she was saying, her eyes downcast quite penitently. 'I know I don't make a very good companion these days, my work and the twins absorbing all my energy. Even now I'm on edge, wondering what the boys have been up to in my absence.'

'Surely they'll be asleep?' Iain led the way to the reception desk to settle the bill.

'One can never tell with those two.' Yet Mary glowed a little, thinking of them. 'They share the incredible imagination of a Picasso!'

'Are they alike in all respects?'

'Who?' she asked, a bit befuddled. 'The twins or Picasso? Oh, I see what you mean!' She stood aside until Iain had retrieved his gold card, then, 'It's impossible to tell,' she continued. 'I never know which is the mischievous ringleader and which the dedicated follower. I think they are each as bad as the other really!'

'But you're glad you have them?' Iain pocketed his wallet after returning the card to it, then, looking directly at her, his expression was one of wonder, for suddenly her eyes were shining as never before and a heartwarming exuberance of emotion beautified her still rather peaky face.

'"Glad" is not a word that could even remotely describe the way I feel about them,' she declared dreamily. 'I'm forever giving thanks for the treasure Robert left behind for me. . .'

Iain's deep-set gold-flecked hazel eyes were equally full of feeling as his rapt gaze dwelt on her spellbound look. For a moment he was silent, then. . . 'You know,' he remarked as they walked out to his car together, 'I wasn't particularly impressed by you at the job interview—I think I was more annoyed than anything—however, I now realise there's a lot more to you than meets the eye, although I have also to admit that you have me confounded, even confused.'

He opened the car door for her then walked round to the driver's side, and, looking over the car roof towards her, asked in a surprisingly appealing and pensive way, 'Don't you want to know anything about me?'

She shook her head, then, when both were seated in the car, she explained, 'I knew from the question you put to me at my interview that one could presuppose you to have a sexist tendency, a wish to keep the little woman bustling at home among domestic chores and children, leaving ideas of careers and such high-minded things to her so-called "better-half" while she panders to his every wish, her single purpose being to keep herself attractive for when he returns home tired from a day's work, no matter how hard she herself has been working all the hours he's been away.'

Iain straightened abruptly. 'Are you a feminist?' he asked, appalled.

She gave a short laugh. 'No. I believe men and women should be equal partners, especially in marriage, loving and helping each other, as Robert and I did.'

Then she added a salutary, 'But to refer again to the question you so unfairly asked during my interview—well, since you have tried to make amends tonight, I suppose I must try to forgive and forget?'

By this time both she and Iain were in the car and she had to raise her voice in order to be heard above the starting of the engine.

'I don't know—you still seem to hold that question against me, in spite of my apology,' he said, sounding irritated.

'You haven't let me finish what I was saying. I was about to add that, realising you probably have as many foibles as anyone else, also that I shall be having to work with you, it seems to me that the less I know about you, and them, the better. To start with, anyway. . .'

'Words of wisdom, or are you still implying that I prejudged you unfairly at the interview?'

'Well, you certainly wouldn't have asked a male applicant what you asked me!'

Grunting as if seeing the humour in her reply, nevertheless he drove on in silence.

Mary, however, experienced a sense of triumph. Robert, she told herself, would have appreciated the way she had managed to stall off any more questions from Iain, for hadn't she played very much the same sort of game with him when they'd first met?

In those days, however, her object had been to attract, not put off! She sighed, deeply, wishing with all her heart that she had not wasted even those few moments of their getting to know one another when they were to have so little time together anyway.

And, thinking this way about Robert, she tried

to put Iain out of her mind, while he for his
part seemed preoccupied in his thoughts, so the
remainder of the journey to the flat passed without another word being spoken by either of them.

Finally, he dropped her off beside the steps
leading to her front door and, after remaining
solicitously watching from his car until she had
safely passed through into her porch, drove off.

Waiting a moment before proceeding further
into the flat, Mary stood wondering at the sudden
sense of loss she felt, almost as if she missed still
having him beside her. She dismissed the unexpected sensation as nonsense, helped by Debbie-Ann
coming out into the narrow hall calling excitedly,
'I've a flight booked! There's been a cancellation
and my travel agent, a good friend, phoned then
booked it for me. I fly off tomorrow!'

Her exuberance slumped suddenly. 'But I'm
worried, Mary,' she confessed. 'Little Rob looked
flushed this evening. I hope he's not sickening for
something. Would you rather I cancelled my trip?'

'No, of course not. He'd probably been pillow-
fighting too long and too hard. Besides, I can
cope, you know that.' After all, I am his mother,
Mary longed to point out, but refrained, not wanting to hurt Debbie-Ann's feelings.

'How is Richie?' she asked instead.

'Oh, he's fine. It's only Rob I'm bothered
about. I had Andrew take a look at him. He was
a little puzzled but said it might just be a cold
coming on.'

'Have you packed?' Mary wanted to change the
subject, something inside her having turned cold

at the mere possibility of anything being wrong with either one of her precious sons.

'Packed?' Debbie-Ann repeated. 'Well, sort of! But Andrew hasn't been gone long. I wanted to get in touch with you but had no way of knowing where you were. You didn't say where you were phoning from and I forgot to ask until you'd rung off.'

'I didn't know where I was, either. I just went where I was taken. Tell you all about it later, but now I want to take a peep at Rob. Don't come with me, will you, or we might disturb him? I won't put his light on, I've a small pencil light in my handbag—that will do.' Mary took it out ready to use.

Quietly she crept to Rob's side, held a hand close to his face and listened to his breathing. She could feel heat rising from his head so very gently pulled back the bedcover, leaving him covered with just a sheet, to help him cool off.

'He is rather hot,' she said when back in the kitchen. 'If he gets any hotter I'll give him some paracetamol syrup. Has he complained of a sore throat?'

'Not to me,' said Debbie-Ann. 'Look, if you're worried about him, perhaps you'd rather I didn't go away tomorrow?'

'It's good of you to offer to stay, Debbie-Ann, but you must go. You ought to take the chance to visit your parents, especially now your father's ill. I only wish circumstances allowed me to visit my Mum and Dad.'

Debbie-Ann studied the lines of anxiety

deepening on Mary's face. 'At least you'll have a doctor looking after the boys,' she said by way of consolation. 'Andrew's sharing with a friend at the moment but has to move out by the weekend, so depends upon moving in here. He can, can't he? After all, neither you nor he could afford to pay for him to live anywhere else.'

'That's true, and in any case I more or less promised he could come here as a temporary measure until he moves into hospital accommodation when he starts his job in the Royal Glen. He'll have a flat of his own then, or at least a share in one.'

Nodding agreement, Debbie-Ann hurried with her packing, anxious to tidy her room ready for Andrew to take over after she left, Mary following to give her a hand.

'He's coming with me in the taxi to the airport in the morning,' Debbie-Ann said, becoming cheerful again. 'Says he'll help me carry my luggage. Thoughtful, isn't he?'

'I think you think he has all the virtues,' Mary teased, helping to reach down another case from the top of a wardrobe. 'If you're taking so many clothes you'll certainly need Andrew to help carry the cases!'

'Clever of me to think of that, wasn't it?' Debbie-Ann grinned. 'In fact I even hinted he might like to come along!'

'You really are falling for him, aren't you?' Mary said gently, adding a fervent, 'Oh, Debbie-Ann, I do hope things go well for you.'

'After your sad experience of an over-short

romance,' Debbie-Ann returned quietly, 'I can't see the sense in wasting time. I only hope Andrew will agree!'

Mary lowered her eyes, overcome with the fear that Debbie-Ann might one day face something of the heartbreak she herself was still suffering, a heartbreak she would not wish on anyone. Even the merest reminder of it allowed anguish to once again break out through the locked door of her heart.

Yet, and she paused wonderingly, even a little guiltily, recalling the strange feelings Iain was able to arouse. Iain, of all people. . .yet she didn't even like him. . .did she?

CHAPTER FIVE

'How's Rob today?' Andrew called back to Mary as he hustled Debbie-Ann down the front steps and into the waiting taxi the next morning.

'OK,' Mary answered simply, not wanting to detain their leaving or to alarm Debbie-Ann by admitting she had been up half the night watching over Rob, sponging him down time and time again in an effort to help lower his temperature, giving him paracetamol syrup, fearing for him in her ever-rising anxiety over his rapidly worsening condition, and finally even carrying him into her own bedroom and putting him into her bed so that his twin would not be disturbed by all the movement going on.

She had spent the rest of the night, at least what little there was left of it, sitting uncomfortably upright on a small dressing-table stool which gave her back no support and left her aching in all her bones.

Nevertheless, no sooner had she waved Debbie off than she was on the phone to her GP asking her to visit Rob as a matter of urgency. The doctor arrived within ten minutes to find Rob already complaining that his neck hurt, refusing to allow even Mary to flex it, and also objecting to the sunlight filtering into his room, his eyes unable to bear any bright light.

He grew drowsier by the second, so, agreeing with Mary that it probably was meningitis, the GP gave him an injection of benzyl penicillin and ordered an emergency ambulance.

Grabbing her coat and handbag, after rushing Richie from his bed and dressing him then providing him with a packet of biscuits and a small carton of orange juice, Mary penned a note briefing Andrew as to what was happening and stuck it where he would be sure to see it by the front door.

In the ambulance Rob immediately started vomiting then fitting, so it was decided to take him to the Royal Glen, as that was the nearest hospital to his home.

Even so, he was unconscious by the time they reached there, so was taken into the resuscitation-room in Casualty where Iain and some nurses awaited him, having been alerted by the GP over her mobile phone as she continued on her visiting round.

The quick glance Iain gave Mary as she handed Rob over into casualty care could have meant anything, but she, in her natural distress and anxiety, took it to be, 'There, just like the fear I expressed at your interview, your children will take pride of place with you in any emergency, to the detriment of your work.'

He was sure, she thought, to be considering himself right in his personal desire not to offer her the staff-doctor job. So she ignored him, her distress deepening when she found Richie and herself shepherded off into the relatives' room as if mere spare parts in Rob's trauma.

Longing to be with him, to comfort and cheer him if possible, she sat on the edge of a chair wondering what she could do to gain recognition of the fact that she was not only his mother, but a doctor in her own right who would soon be taking over as one of the seniors of the very casualty department she was sitting in at that moment. She could hardly say so to anyone, she decided, or she might start the job at a disadvantage, putting backs up by appearing to want to throw her weight about.

Frustrated, she waited, finding a comic for Richie to look at until a clerk came in to ask questions and write down the answers.

'Your GP's name?' she wanted to know.

Mary gave it.

'Religion?' she was asked next.

Befuddled, Mary replied, 'I've no idea what her religion is.'

'The patient's religion, I mean, not the GP's!' The girl sighed frustratedly as if exasperated by the dumbness of some people.

Mary pulled herself together, then, when the questionnaire was duly finished, the clerk left and another person came in to see her and ask further questions. Mary felt everyone must be thinking her a hopeless ignoramus, she was having medical things explained to her in such detail. When would they let her go to Rob? That was all she wanted. Yet how could she leave Richie by himself to worry and fret over what was happening to his twin? She noticed he showed little interest in the comic.

She turned to him, aware that he had been strangely silent since she had roused him from his sleep, had not touched his biscuits or the drink, but had simply watched, big-eyed, taking in all that was happening to his twin in the ambulance and since.

She put an arm around him, cuddling him to her. 'Rob will be all right,' she assured him, wishing she felt as certain as she tried to sound.

Then a nurse came in, followed, to Mary's great relief, by Andrew.

'Debbie-Ann sent me back from the airport *post-haste*,' he said before the nurse could get a word in. 'She was still worrying about Rob, so after reading your note I came to take Richie off your hands and drop him off at playschool. I was lucky: came across a medic friend whose old man runs a garage. They've lent me a car for a few days!'

'You can come along to Resus. with me if you wish,' the nurse said to Mary then, so she bade a hasty goodbye to Richie and Andrew and went off with her.

'I should warn you,' said the nurse as they walked along the corridor together, 'your little boy has a drip up and is "fitting" so the consultant has given him some anaesthetic.' Then, still under the misapprehension that Mary would know little of medical procedures, she added, 'You'll see a tube coming out of his mouth, helping him to breathe. . .'

'You mean that Iain's intubated him?' Mary said without thinking, surprising the nurse, who was even more taken aback when Iain came to meet them, saying to her, 'By the way, this lady——' he nodded solemnly towards Mary '—is our new staff-grade doctor. She joins us at the beginning of next month.'

'Oh, I'm sorry!' The nurse retired in confusion in spite of the understanding smile Mary managed to raise.

'You should have made yourself known,' Iain said rebukingly, going on to tell Mary that, the paediatric nursing staff being caught up in another emergency on their ward, he had arranged a bed in Intensive Care for Rob, who would be going there as soon as the porter arrived to take him.

She watched Rob being put on the portable ventilator attached to the trolley and saw Iain check up on the antibiotics and dosage already given, then, turning to her, he remarked that it was very helpful to have had them given to Rob so early that morning.

He really cares, she found herself thinking, frequently glancing towards his tense face while walking along to Intensive Care with him together with the porter and the nurse, but once there, fearing she would again be parted from Rob, she forgot everything except to impress upon Iain that she wanted to be with and hold her sick son while the necessary lumbar puncture was being done, so that he would know she was there. And I won't faint, she promised herself, I just won't faint, not even if anyone expects me to!

Which of course was a reference to Iain most of all. However, another doctor did the lumbar puncture, and, watching, Mary went cold. 'It does look rather cloudy, doesn't it?' she managed to murmur haltingly even while endeavouring to hide her mounting fears because of being only too well aware that the cloudiness of the CSF—the fluid surrounding the spinal cord—was indeed one of the signs of meningitis.

'Yes,' the doctor replied in a colourless voice while continuing with his task. 'I'm afraid it is cloudy.'

Fighting to control her distress, nevertheless Mary walked away looking for a corner in which to hide, knowing she needed to cry; but to her great surprise she almost bumped into Andrew and Richie.

'I didn't expect you to get back yet. Rob's in Intensive Care,' she gulped, her chin quivering and her eyes screwing themselves up in an attempt to stop what threatened to be a sudden flood of tears.

'Don't give way—you're needed.' Andrew slipped a comforting arm about her shoulders. 'Have trust, Mary. He'll be all right. A doctor's giving the whole playgroup preventative medicine, so as Richie's had his I was allowed to pop him over here because he wanted to give you a cuddle.'

'Which is just what I need most.' Mary was already picking him up and hugging him close.

'Why did everyone have to drink Rob's medicine?' Richie asked into her ear, adding a puzzled, 'Why didn't he drink it himself?'

'I expect he'd had his,' replied Mary. 'What sort of medicine was it?'

'Pink,' said Richie, then darted away from her to climb over some piled up chairs, so Andrew went after him to keep him safe then take him back to the playgroup, while Mary phoned Mr Drew to tell him about Rob's illness.

'Stay with him as long as you feel it necessary,' he said sympathetically. 'We'll cover your duties here.'

So she spent another night sitting in a chair beside Rob's bed, this time a bed in Intensive Care. An uncomfortable night by any standards, but all she wanted was to be with him.

The next day, Intensive Care specialists told her they were going to reduce Rob's sedation to see if he could breathe for himself without fitting, and—giving her some much-needed hope—added that tests had shown that the bacterial meningitis was sensitive to penicillin, so the treatment the GP had started so early had been absolutely correct, and of great help.

By midday Rob was recognising Mary, but the tube in his mouth prevented him from talking; however, before the evening came the tube was taken out and Richie was allowed to visit him for just a couple of minutes, then Andrew took Richie back to the flat.

Iain had popped in to see Rob from time to time, and although apparently satisfied all was going well with him, from the shrewd glances he gave Mary it was obvious he was growing very concerned about her herself.

'Have you been getting enough to eat?' he asked eventually. 'You've that starved look on your face and it worries me. Come along to the canteen; I'll stand you a decent meal. I don't suppose you brought any money with you, did you?'

Mary tried thinking up excuses, not wanting to admit that he was right. Money had been the last thing she had thought about when preparing to accompany Rob in the ambulance.

Iain took her by the elbow, making her rise from her chair. 'Hopefully Rob will sleep for some time now,' he said, 'so there's no point in your running your own health down and getting yourself exhausted. Come along. I haven't any time to waste, and I won't go without you. You can choose the meal you want then I'll come back here and stay with Rob while you eat it. Be sensible, now.'

Giving a lingering, longing look back to the sleeping Rob, Mary rose obediently and followed Iain out into the corridor. Not that she wanted to; she would have much preferred to stay beside Rob but knew Iain was talking sense and that she would need to remain fit for when she had to return to work, besides taking extra care of her twins.

She walked slowly, not really wanting to catch up with Iain as that might involve having to think up something to say and her brain was too tired to bother.

But Iain turned, waited and smiled one of his special smiles, putting new life into her. 'It's been a very tough couple of days for you, hasn't it?' he remarked with an understanding she had not expected. 'Andrew is being helpful, I believe?'

Mary nodded, still incapable of hurrying. 'I don't know what I would do without him,' she said, and was surprised to see Iain frown.

He said nothing more, however, until they queued at the canteen counter and he had paid for the dish of lasagne he recommended her to try, although she still protested against having anything at all.

'You must eat, Mary,' he insisted in his forceful way, 'and, I warn you, I'll come back and expect to see your plate empty.'

So finally, left without enough energy to argue, she accepted the lasagne then sat just looking at it while he returned to Rob.

Inwardly rebelling and determined not give in to him, nevertheless while Mary waited a thought struck her. What if Iain considered her lackadaisical mood a permanent impediment and tried to persuade the powers that be to withdraw the staff-grade offer? Could they? In her extreme weariness and state of anxiety over Rob, she was quite ready to believe anything gloomy, however unlikely.

So, making an enormous effort, she ate a few forkfuls of lasagne and braced herself to appear lively when Iain joined her at the table saying Rob was sleeping well and was under first-rate medical care so there was no need for her to hurry back to him.

'But I want to,' she demurred, 'and I've eaten

all I can—just as you recommended. I feel fine again!'

'Very well,' he sighed, a frown of frustration again spoiling his former good-tempered expression. 'I'll go back to my department, then.' And without more ado he left her.

Did I overact? wondered Mary. Will he be thinking I don't really care about Rob? Oh no, surely not! and, more disturbed than ever, she found her own way back to Intensive Care.

Late as it was, Andrew brought Richie in to say goodnight to her, then he too seemed struck by her obvious fatigue. 'In all fairness to young Richie, I think you should take him back to the flat and spend the night there with him, while I take over here and stay beside Rob,' he suggested persuasively. 'After all, Rob seems over the worst of it now, and you certainly won't be fit to look after him when he gets home if you're going to continue like this! You're badly in need of a decent night's sleep, Mary, and it's up to you to get it.'

Seeing the sense in his proposal, Mary agreed and stayed at home that night so that Richie would not feel left out in any way.

The next day Rob was so much better that he was transferred to the ordinary paediatric ward and Mary was able to work in her hospital for a few hours while Richie was at playschool, Andrew taking him there and back, helpfully spending the rest of the day clearing up the flat between his visits to Rob. Then, for the next couple of days—her stress lessening—she spent the

evenings with Rob but nights in the flat with
Richie, Andrew sleeping in a reclining chair by
Rob's bed in the ward.

Finally, after six days in hospital, Rob was able
to go home, declared fit and well, and instead
of yielding to temptation and crying all over
him in her great relief, Mary decided to throw
a party.

She was planning the details when Iain walked
over to her in her hospital canteen and sat beside
her. To her own great surprise, she heard herself
giving him the first invitation. She couldn't seem
to stop the words coming out.

Iain seemed equally surprised.

'A party?' His eyebrows shot up expressively
high. 'Why, what are you celebrating?' he asked.

'Lots of things,' Mary replied enthusiastically,
'Rob's recovery, for a start, also Andrew and I
getting our new jobs, and Debbie-Ann, my real
helper, returning from South Africa—at least, she
should be returning by the time I have the party
organised. I also feel a need to have a farewell
do for the casualty staff I'll be leaving behind,
and a welcome do for the staff I'll be joining—
oh, and I'd wish to include a special thank you
to the Intensive Care staff of the Royal Glen hospital who were so good with Rob.' She paused
for breath.

'Also I'd invite all the doctors, nurses, porters
and cleaning staff of the Accident and Emergency
departments of both hospitals,' she added when
she could, 'Plus the children and leaders from the
playgroup because Rob and Richie will be leaving

there and starting at kindergarten after the holidays.'

Taking a second breath, 'You know, it seems quite incredible to have the twins coming up to four years of age, as they will be by then. Their babyhood will be left well behind, won't it?' Mary's wistful smile was tinged with regret.

'Have you counted up the number of people you'd be inviting to this party of yours? Could you cater for so many?' Iain scowled a little scornfully.

'I'm sure I'd get plenty of willing help,' Mary replied, immediately on the defensive as she usually was with him. 'Andrew, for one, would be sure to rally round. I know I can depend on him to support me. He doesn't pick holes in everything I want to do, not like you,' she claimed, her aggravation driving her.

'And where would you put everyone?' Iain scoffed. 'Your flat would burst at the seams.'

'I was thinking I might ask permission to use the hospital grounds.'

'And if it rains, everyone will be put up in the wards?' He smiled mockingly.

'I regret having mentioned the party at all. You're taking all the fun out of it!' Mary remonstrated indignantly. 'I don't know why you came to the canteen today and bothered to sit beside me when all you seem to want to do is throw cold water over my ideas.'

'My coming to this hospital today was purely to do with work. . .and why I came over to sit with you was a gesture of common courtesy, that's all. You looked lonely sitting there by yourself with just the inevitable cup of tea keeping you company.' And without another word or even a vestige of encouragement softening either his voice or suddenly granite-like face, he pushed his chair back and stood up.

'I was beginning to think we might be friends,' he claimed rather sourly. 'However, I see I was wrong. I wonder you even bothered to mention the proposed party to me. Were you trying to prove something to yourself?'

'Such as?' Mary challenged.

He shrugged. 'Who knows?' he questioned. 'I certainly don't!' Then, looking quite furious, he strode away and out of the canteen.

'I confess I was very disappointed in him,' Mary admitted later to Gabrielle, telling her the whole story. 'He's an old misery!'

Then, leaving Gabrielle, she returned to the front of Casualty and, dismissing Iain from her thoughts, worked speedily and well, seeing one person after another, most of them having come in with commonplace complaints.

Soon the doctors' box was empty of patients' cards, the majority of people having simply needed a first treatment by nurses, together with advice on how to prevent a recurrence of whatever troubled them if there was nothing seriously wrong.

Eventually there were only two patients left in the department except for those in the short-stay ward, but one of the two, a very excited small boy, was hanging back to proudly show off his bandaged finger to the elderly man remaining in one of the cubicles, and the completely mystified expression on the boy's face when the man produced an equally well-bandaged finger of his own reminded Mary of her own boys so, relaxing, her spirits raised, she laughed and went back into the department's little kitchen to sit at the table and write up her notes.

'All that frantic activity earlier,' Gabrielle commented, following her in. 'You've certainly been on the go! I knew someone had been ruffling your feathers just by the look on your face when you returned from the canteen earlier on. In fact I shivered in my shoes for you when I saw the Royal Glen's casualty consultant go in after you.'

'And didn't you see him come out again, his scowl enough to sour the milk in his tea?'

Before she could say anything more, Mary was alerted by a noise. 'Listen!' she exclaimed. 'The blinds are being pulled around the resuscitation entrance! I wonder what's up?'

Leaving everything just as it was, the two girls rushed along to offer their help.

CHAPTER SIX

'A NEAR-FATAL tragedy,' they were informed. 'A young girl's jacket caught in the door of a bus as it drove off, pulling her along!'

The girl was conscious on arrival, trying to talk but obviously in great pain. The caught jacket had held her up, fortunately, preventing her from being dragged under the wheels of the bus, but it was several seconds before the driver's attention was caught by the mother's screams and bangs on the door as, running beside it, she fought frantically hard to attract his attention and have him stop the bus; but by that time her daughter had been badly injured. . .

Upon examination she was found to have extensive damage to soft tissues and bone of one leg, with deep grazes on the other leg and to one hand.

Speedily Mary and the resuscitation team put in intravenous cannulae, connected the girl to oxygen and the monitors to take blood for cross-matching and testing. . .and then the X-ray team came in to do their part of the work.

By this time Staff Nurse Gabrielle and the other nurses had wrapped the badly injured leg in sterile green towels and the young girl had been given the painkiller diamorphine; also she was given a couple of units of haemaccel—fluid replacement—besides having chest, pelvic and leg X-rays taken.

Then, having been referred to the orthopaedic and plastic surgeons, she was taken to them in Theatre.

'Her mother hasn't stopped crying long enough for us to find out whether her daughter suffers from any allergies,' Mary was told by an anxious registrar. 'She's very distressed but managed to sign that she knows you and wants to talk to you, Mary. See what you can find out from her, will you, and—don't tell her until it's certain—but the orthopods think there's a chance they'll be able to save the damaged leg.'

Considerably cheered by news of the possibility, Mary went to the relatives' room and seated herself beside the weeping mother, greeting her and mentioning that she remembered their meeting while delivering children to the same playschool, then, taking her hand in hers, her very attitude exuding sympathy, she asked about allergies and tetanus.

'No, no allergies and yes, she's had her tetanus injections,' gulped the mother even in the midst of her misery and muddled confusion, so the nurse accompanying Mary passed on the crucial information to the registrar, leaving Mary to try to console the young mother in her almost hysterical distress over the accident.

'I banged and banged on the driver's door but he couldn't hear me,' she kept repeating over and over again. 'He had just started off. I was on the pavement, you see, and couldn't reach Michaela no matter how I tried. . .oh, it was awful. . .it wasn't possible to pull her away in time, her jacket was caught in the door, there was nothing she could do and nothing I could do to help her!'

'It was a good thing the jacket was so well caught up,' Mary put in quietly. 'It saved Michaela from being pulled under the wheels, so that's something to be thankful for. . .'

But she was not being listened to; the mother's need to talk had suddenly become paramount.

'I'd just left Simon in playschool. I'm glad he wasn't there to see what happened. Oh, it's all so terrible—what can I do?' Completely distraught, she broke down again so Mary slipped a compassionate arm about her.

'Michaela's such a lovely girl; supposing she dies!' the mother continued when she could after giving way to a storm of tears. 'I'd never be able to forgive myself for not saving her, never, never. . .life simply wouldn't be worth living!'

Mary hugged her. 'But she isn't dead, and just remember your little Simon too,' she urged gently. 'He'll need comforting, and so will your husband. Look, give the nurse the name and phone number of a relative or friend you'd like to come to be with you. A nurse will bring you a cup of tea meanwhile. And please stay cheerful and hopeful, for everyone's sake, especially your daughter's. I'd like to stay with you but I can't. I've other patients waiting to be seen, but I'll come back when I can. . .'

Michaela's mother looked up at her with

tearswept doe-like eyes, and it was hard to ignore the stab of pathos they aroused, but Mary, concerned for the other patients who had arrived while the injured girl was being attended to, and out of fairness to them, hurried back to her casualty department, leaving a nurse to attend to the mother. . .

To her surprise she met Iain on the way.

'I've been wanting to talk to you,' he began, reaching out a hand to catch her arm as she attempted to get past.

She jerked out of his hold. 'I can't stop now, I'm busy,' she demurred, making to walk on.

'Then I'll come round to your flat. Seven-thirty suit you?'

'I'll be bathing the boys and settling them off for the night.'

'Isn't that someone else's job?'

'It's mine tonight. Look, I've got to go!'

'Seven-thirty,' he insisted imperiously.

'It's my hair-shampooing night,' she declared firmly.

'I'm adept at towelling,' he maintained dogmatically, standing tall. . .then walked on.

Trying not to be aggravated, and unable to think up a suitably snappy reply, Mary was glad to be distracted by the extraordinary sight of a six- or seven-year-old boy crawling over the floor while carefully keeping his left knee from touching it.

'What's all this in aid of?' she asked, trying not to look amused, the boy's expression being so serious.

'My knee hurt but it's getting better now,' he told her solemnly.

'Let's have a look at it,' she urged.

'No, 'cos it's all right now,' he assured her solemnly.

His mother butted in. 'He rarely complains about knocks and things,' she put in on his behalf, 'he's so mad on sports, so I don't know why he's taken to crawling. At his age, I ask you! But I'm beginning to wonder whether something went into his knee and came out again. He wouldn't be likely to say.'

But in her pleasant way Mary finally persuaded him to let her examine the knee. She found it red, hot and with a knee effusion, showing there was fluid in the knee joint. Also she discovered a tiny pinprick mark.

Asking him whether he could remember pricking it with anything but receiving only a determinedly negative shake of the head in reply, she decided to have an X-ray taken, and was glad she had when she saw that he had to be transported to the X-ray department in a wheelchair as bending the knee made him bite his lips in pain.

The X-ray showed there was a full needle in his knee, the point having broken off and lodged in the knee joint.

'I'm afraid you'll have to stay in hospital for a few days,' she said, then wondered why, when he appeared to be so brave, he immediately clung to his mother's hand as if to a lifeline.

'I'm sorry, young man,' she said sympathetically, 'but we simply must get rid of the infection in your knee and draw the needle out; you'll have terrible trouble with it otherwise and a great deal of pain. It must be hurting you like mad now. . . it is, isn't it? How did it get there?'

'I don't know. I think I fell on it,' he half whispered his reply.

And from the scared look in his intelligent eyes, Mary guessed he had already realised that his knee would need hospital treatment, yet for some reason he would rather put up with any amount of pain rather than stay in hospital, so was trying to convince his mother and himself that there was nothing wrong with his knee.

But at Mary's words his show of bravado broke down and he wept, still clinging to his mother and she realised that he had a deep-seated fear of being parted from her.

However, by dint of kindly reassuring questioning, she discovered the cause of his fear. Apparently his father had walked out of the family home a few months earlier and had never come back.

'I cried a lot when Dad said he was going,' the boy sobbed, going on to confess that he had thought that was why his father had never returned. 'He didn't like me crying, you see. I shouldn't have done it, then he might have stayed.'

Listening to him and witnessing the hurt and fear deep in his eyes, Mary realised that, to him, going into hospital carried a very real risk of his mother leaving him as well.

'So that's how things are.' Listening, his mother

put a loving arm around him. 'It seems I've been too engrossed in my own misery to pay much attention to his. I told you he never complains, Doctor. It's really been quite uncanny.'

'I don't think there's any doubt but that he is really worried that you might disappear out of his life if he has to stay in hospital,' Mary stressed when the boy had been taken along to be seen by the orthopaedic doctor.

'As if I would leave him! It would break my heart, I love him so. Oh, Doctor, how can I make him realise I would stay with him, no matter what?' the mother asked tearfully.

'Reassure him by remaining with him in hospital; you can be together in the ward all day and all night. . .every day, every night, if you wish. You could even help look after him yourself.'

'It's allowed?' The boy's mother brightened. 'It wasn't when I was a child!'

'Things have changed.' Mary smiled, then, having sorted out the boy's problem to his satisfaction, she found her mind turning to her own fatherless twins, wondering how they were to fare in life with only a mother to bring them up, and a fully career-occupied mother at that.

Would they come to resent the fact that they had no father? And would that resentment one day develop into burdensome chips to be carried on their shoulders for the rest of their lives?

Which was the very theme Iain seemed keen on expanding when he called on her that evening.

He made himself at home, followed her into

the kitchen and asked when the hair-washing experience was to begin.

'Hair-washing experience indeed!' Mary repeated after him. 'As if I would want any man to see me with my hair all damp and stringy!'

'Oh, I don't know.' He looked at her thoughtfully. 'Some people can even look good in ill-fitting RTA emergency clothing!'

Which of course made her blush, remembering the dishevelled picture she must have presented upon her return from the terrible trauma of the trapped motorist.

Iain put a hand on her shoulder, a warm hand yet it made a sort of shiver run through her. She wriggled out of his reach. 'Would you like a cup of tea?' she asked a little breathlessly, angry with herself for her reaction to his touch.

Robert's was the only touch she had wanted, she reminded herself with a catch in her throat. The only touch she had ever wanted. Yet now here was Iain Stewart thoroughly disturbing her equilibrium merely by placing a hand on her shoulder. . .having the same effect on her as when he had inadvertently touched her neck when passing behind her in the canteen. . .that day she had joined Mr Drew and himself at their table.

'This, I suppose, is your wedding photo?' he was saying, standing in front of the framed photograph gracing the narrow iron mantelpiece. 'You made a very pretty bride.' Then he added, so quietly that she could scarcely distinguish the words, 'It's no wonder your Robert seemed so proud of you, and so very happy.'

Mary was choked up and quite unable to speak. She wanted to ask what he would like to have to eat or whether perhaps he had already had his meal, but it was as if her tongue were tied. She filled the little electric kettle with water, switched it on and stood close by it with her back to Iain.

He came and stood behind her, so close that she could feel the warmth of him. It disturbed her.

'You were deeply in love with your Robert, weren't you?' he murmured softly. 'He was a very lucky man.'

Mary started up, anger flooding through her, helping her find her voice. 'Lucky?' she echoed with some bitterness. 'Lucky to have loved and lost, is that what you're saying?'

'You know I didn't mean it in that way. Lucky to have had your love, that was what I was meaning.'

'How do you know what I was like with him? Perhaps our love was too strong, too passionate to last. I might have disappointed him, he might have disappointed me. . .I'll never know, will I? So don't say he was lucky to have had my love, and don't say I was lucky to have had his. . .it was all too short-lived, and I just can't bear to think of the years I've missed with him if what we had between us might have lasted.'

The kettle boiled, spluttered, but neither Iain nor Mary took any notice. Once or twice Iain's arm went out as if wanting to enfold Mary, but he never let it stray that far, drawing it back to his side a little guiltily each time as if hoping she had not noticed.

He need not have worried. She was in no mood to pay regard to anything but her own misery, and the fact that she was feeling guilty, although her self-reproach was due more to the fact that her raw feelings were being displayed to the one person she had inwardly pledged herself to dislike.

What would the autocratic, self-opinionated Iain Stewart know about emotions that could carry one sky-high one minute and plunge one down into the depths the next? Granted, he could show a nice side of himself occasionally, but the other and more usual side of him was dark, dismal and compelling, therefore much to be avoided at all times and at all costs, since it brought nothing but a strange painful yearning in its wake.

'What's the matter, Mary?' he asked, his tone tender, but tenderness was the last thing she could tolerate at that moment.

'Nothing's the matter; why should there be anything?' she asked brusquely.

He took hold of one of the wooden kitchen chairs, swung it round and sat down straddling his legs across the seat, his arms folded across the back of the chair.

'You know, Mary Mary quite contrary, I think you should give serious thought to marrying again,' he said. 'After all, you're young, quite attractive—perhaps more than "quite", and have the twins to consider. Where are they, by the way?'

'Asleep. They went to bed early, having been up since six,' she answered crisply, not wanting to admit that she had put them to bed extra early just in case he did turn up. Not that she had wanted to ensure more time alone with him, she assured herself, working up feelings of resentment instead.

She paused, tea-making quite forgotten. 'You think I should marry again? Is that your fond hope, a way of getting me out of your department before I have even had a chance to start there? I didn't realise your disapproval of me went that far!'

'You do me an injustice. I had no such thought or idea in my mind. It just seems such a pity for you to have to live as you are living when things could be made so much easier for you.'

'Thank you,' Mary said coldly. 'But I think I'm quite old enough to make my own decisions in life. I don't need any suggestions or supervision. In fact——' she turned to him then, her eyes stormy '—if you called round simply to criticise and make your own assumptions, false ones at that, then I'm afraid I must ask you to leave so that I can get on with the things I want to do.'

'Such as shampooing your hair?'

She shrugged indifferently. 'Perhaps.'

He stood up. 'I still don't know how to get through to you. I seem to say all the wrong things. Perhaps it would be better if I left.' He walked to the door. 'We still don't know much about each other, do we?' he commented sourly.

Still aggrieved, 'No,' snapped Mary, 'and at this rate we won't be finding out anything more.' She hesitated, feeling ashamed of her grumpiness and remembering that she would soon be working with him in the Royal Glen hospital. . .

'I'm sorry,' she added, 'but you do seem to have caught me on a bad day. I've had to deal with some very difficult cases and I'm tired out. We shall have to learn to get on with each other I suppose, or the atmosphere in your A and E department will be quite unbearable.'

She paused, to continue thoughtfully, 'I suppose a partnership such as ours in Casualty must be like a marriage in a way. . .we shall need to consider each other's points of view and different ways of working, adjust to each other and be prepared to give and take.' She sighed. 'I don't know whether we shall ever find it possible to be that compatible, but I suppose we shall have to try.'

She looked up at him as he stepped back towards her.

'You mean I should give you as much understanding as I should give a wife?' he asked, his face brightening, a quite mischievous look taking over.

Mary stared, never before having noticed how attractive his rather crooked smile could be. Studying it, she forgot to listen to what he was saying until his mention of a wife caught her attention.

'I'm sorry, I didn't catch your last words,' she said, so quietly that it was almost a whisper.

'I was saying that as I've never had a wife I don't really know how to treat one. You will have to be my guinea-pig.'

'I don't know that I like being called a guinea-pig,' Mary muttered, pulling a face, 'but I think I know what you mean, and—all right—I'll give the relationship a try. . .as long as you humour me, acknowledging that I have my own way of doing things, medically speaking, a way that often proves right.'

'Relationship?' Iain queried. 'Oh, you simply mean the relationship between consultant and staff-grade doctor? I hoped you. . .oh, well, never mind what I hoped. . . Now, what about putting fresh water in that kettle and making tea?'

Wondering if the colour in her cheeks would ever quieten down and still rather bemused, nevertheless, 'What would you like to have with your cup of tea?' Mary managed to ask at long last, the question having been hovering at the back of her mind ever since he walked in and she first put the kettle on, which, she thought wryly, was at least a whole quarrel and a half ago!

'What have you to offer?' Iain was answering, the impish gleam still in his eye, just as there came the sound of a key turning in the front door lock and Andrew walked in without as much as a warning knock.

On seeing him, the change in Iain's expression was quite remarkable!

CHAPTER SEVEN

ALTHOUGH it was impossible to dismiss the effect Iain had had upon her, Mary refused to allow her mind to dwell on it, instead making light of what had happened when Andrew arrived, and telling Gabrielle about that, although not about what had happened just before. . .

'Oh, you should have seen how flabbergasted Iain Stewart looked at the sight of Andrew coming in loaded with shopping and, after only the briefest acknowledgement of our presence, unpacking groceries and sorting them away as if he was the owner of the place, obviously very much at home,' she said. 'Not for the life of me could I think of any explanation I could offer to make the position clearer; I was too intent on watching to see what was going to happen!'

'And what did?'

'Well, Andrew had brought in two pizzas for our supper and apparently without thought set just two places at the little table. Iain stood and watched, obviously trying to figure out Andrew's position in my household and gloweringly disliking the conclusion he drew.'

'And you?' Gabrielle prompted.

'Oh, me? I was still all on edge inside, sure he had got it all wrong and wondering which of us would break the ice and be the first to make some appropriate comment.'

'So, what happened?' Gabrielle finished checking over the emergency trolley, making sure it had every necessity ready in case a seriously ill or injured patient might be brought in.

'Well,' Mary continued, 'Andrew offered to share his pizza with Iain who said no, he wouldn't dream of depriving him of any of it, then left.

'Actually Andrew was quite upset,' Mary continued in a surprised tone. 'Kept moaning about the impossibility of living such an unfortunate happening down, and declaring it was a good thing he wasn't going to work in Iain Stewart's department.

'Not wanting him to blame Iain all that much, I said I didn't think he'd have anything to fear as Mr Stewart didn't strike me as someone who would bear grudges or anything in that line. However, Andrew wasn't to be so easily pacified, maintaining that Iain would hate his guts and show it, which I have to say I thought a most unfair indictment.

'"Yes, he'd hate my guts and it would show," he repeated rather sulkily, which was not like him at all, so I wasn't surprised when he added an apology, only it was to me, not meant for Iain, something about being sorry because he forgot he was addressing a lady! And, becoming his more usual polite and gentlemanly self once more, he explained that what he had meant to imply was that in his opinion Iain Stewart was adopting a very proprietorial air towards me, as if beginning to look on me as his own!

'That's nonsense, we dislike each other, I told him, then, changing topics, told him why I had nearly been too late for my interview. It seems *he* had merely been playing squash while *I'd* had young Matthew to attend to after he'd been knocked off his bike while doing his paper round.'

'Oh, that was terrible.' Gabrielle whitened. 'I didn't think we'd be able to save him, did you?'

'Andrew, sour as he was about Iain, was quite impressed by the speed with which you summoned help, bleeping me out of my bed because there were no other experienced doctors available, and having the resuscitation-room all set up and even meeting me at the casualty door with a green plastic apron and latex gloves as soon as the taxi you'd ordered for me dropped me off.'

'You didn't blame me for calling you in?' Gabrielle interrupted.

'No of course not, you did the right thing,' Mary replied. 'Anyway, I told Andrew you never waste time in these emergencies, and could see he was quite impressed by your speedy reaction.'

Pleased, Gabrielle gave a smug little smile.

'Then I gave him all the gory details relating to the many injuries Matthew had suffered. I spared him nothing.' Mary grinned mischievously. 'I think that while taking a year off from medicine he had forgotten about the sufferings some people have to put up with, so I was determined to make him show interest about someone other than himself, and stop thinking up nonsense about Iain Stewart and me.

'He did sit up and take notice when he realised I had had to take charge because the senior registrar was otherwise engaged, busy resuscitating a patient who'd had a heart attack.

'"Wow, I'm glad I'm not going into A and E," he said. "You never know what you're going to have to tackle next. At least in orthopaedics it's more predictable, one has a list to follow. Anyway, what did you do next?"

'So I told him,' Mary continued. 'Went through the whole rigmarole for his benefit, just in case he had forgotten his earlier essential training in A and E. Said about checking Matthew's eyes and breathing, guiding the ambulance men where best to put him while I checked his circulation and conscious state, also took some of his blood and connected him to a drip of intravenous fluid, got the new SHO to label the phials and send them off to the laboratory for a full blood-count and cross-match, at the same time arranging for a portable X-ray machine to be brought into the resuscitation-room and you, Gabrielle, connecting Matthew to oxygen, also to an automatic blood-pressure and heart monitor, not to mention the pulse oxymeter! Then I checked the pulse in the foot of his broken leg, rechecked his chest and abdomen, in fact did all the things we seem to have to do so often nowadays.' Mary took some deep breaths, then continued, 'But you should have seen Andrew's face as I said all this. One could tell he hadn't had much experience of the hectic activity and strange excitement of life in a busy casualty department; he's only done six months and that in a very quiet unit where they saw very little major trauma, he said.

'Still,' Mary went on, 'he was able to appreciate the anxiety we knew when we found Matthew wouldn't, or couldn't, speak or make any noise at all and discovered his Glasgow coma scale to be only seven, when according to the Glasgow method of scoring someone with a decreased level of consciousness, a seven on the scale is very low.

'By this time I think Andrew was feeling like taking another year out, especially when he heard that one of the new SHOs had fainted when he saw the effects of the head injury, blood coming from everywhere! It was pretty gruesome, wasn't it?' Mary reminded Gabrielle. 'In fact, that SHO was concentrating so much on the head injury, he hadn't noticed the unstable fracture of Matthew's right tibia and fibula, nor realised the probability of pelvic or chest and abdominal injuries. Poor chap, I think he was quite shattered by his first experience in A and E.'

'I know,' Gabrielle agreed, 'I thought he was going to faint, so I made him sit down while the X-rays of Matthew's skull, lateral cervical spine, spine, chest, pelvis and right lower leg were being taken. Did you tell Andrew that Matthew almost died at one point?'

'You mean when he stopped breathing? Wasn't that traumatic? Yes, I told him that all I could do was hope and pray while I rubbed Matthew's sternum in an effort to stimulate him to breathe.'

Mary stayed silent for a moment, her face mirroring the mixture of emotions she had felt at that time.

Then she brightened. 'But wasn't it wonderful when he did start breathing again? I'll never forget the sheer joy and relief that flooded through me after that awful, stressful moment had passed. Then, as I further told Andrew, the anaesthetic registrar I'd called in earlier arrived and was able to paralyse and ventilate the poor boy.

'"And all this happened before your interview?" Andrew gasped, plainly dumbfounded. "Did you tell the Selection Board?"

'No fear! I said. I didn't say more to them than I had to.

'Which was true enough,' she said to Gabrielle, 'but telling Andrew was something different altogether. I wanted him to get a real reminder of what casualty officers have to go through, feeling sure he hadn't allowed himself to remember, so I spared him nothing, even mentioning injecting the necessary drugs through Matthew's canula while he was being given oxygen, and then applying cricoid pressure while the anaesthetist was intubating him and connecting him to the ventilator, besides having to remember to ask a nurse to call the plaster technician to put a long-leg backslab on the broken leg, and get her to arrange for a brain scan.

'"Your mind must have been whirring like a gyroscope," Andrew commented when I also said about calling the surgical registrar to assess whether any abdominal damage had been

sustained, and told him I gave Matthew intravenous antibiotics then checked that the scanning
room was ready, arranged for a porter to wheel
the boy down accompanied by the anaesthetist, a
nurse and myself, and that in spite of all the careful preparations we had to wait because someone
else was still being scanned, and while we waited,
Matthew's bleeding began again, which was very
worrying.

'To cap it all, I told him, no one there could
manage to get a urinary catheter into Matthew,
and if I hadn't had urological experience I don't
think I'd have managed it either.

'Honestly, Gabrielle, I think Andrew almost
ran out of all the whews, oh, I says and oh hecks
and such like exclamations before I'd finished my
recounting, especially when I added that all the
time I was having to see to so many things I was
also supposed to be keeping up all the necessary
paperwork, details of everything having to be
written down in triplicate!

'He seemed impressed, to say the least!'
Mary took more much needed breaths. 'So I
think I achieved what I'd set out to do,' she
went on pensively. 'I don't see why men shouldn't
be made to realise we are just as capable and
dependable in emergencies as they think *they*
are, do you?'

Then she grimaced, adding, 'Oh, dear, if Iain
Stewart had heard me say that, he'd be certain
I'm a feminist in spite of my denial when he more
or less accused me of it recently!

'I suppose I was rather hard on Andrew, telling

him so much, but it served a double purpose, helping me too. I was glad to get it all off my chest because the whole thing had been so dreadfully anguishing.

'What I find so strange is that Andrew didn't appear to have heard of the Glasgow coma scale, perhaps because he'd been away from this country, and medicine, for so long?

'Yet, thinking over what had happened,' she continued, 'perhaps I should have told him that the most exhausting role I had to play this morning was having to be the one to tell Matthew's distressed family about his terrible injuries and the need to transfer him to the Royal Glen because of the specialised treatment he requires.

'They all cried, and I'm afraid I cried with them. It's obviously a very close-knit family, and oh, they'll be so sad if he dies. So shall I.'

'We did all we could for him,' Gabrielle reminded her, tears filling her own eyes.

'I suppose I shouldn't have stayed with them so long, in view of the pending interview,' Mary continued pensively, 'but I wanted to make sure they realised that most of the highly technical equipment they'll find surrounding Matthew is there mainly to enable nurses to keep an eye on his condition without disturbing him.

'I know many people find all the electronic gadgets rather frightening. In fact, I purposely made that point to Andrew afterwards because it seemed to me that he is not all that sensitive or understanding. Sorry, Gabrielle, but it's the truth, isn't it? You'll have to educate him in that direction.' Mary softened her criticism of him with a gentle smile.

'I suppose I was rather hard on him,' she reminisced again, 'especially telling him so much, but the whole thing had all been so very traumatic.

'Anyway,' she continued, 'I didn't tell him much more, only that I'd told the family I hoped to visit Matthew again, with them, when he's in the Royal Glen, then I simply flew to the flat, changed my clothes and raced to get to my interview, not knowing whether I would make it in time, but as it happened I just scraped in!'

'Mr Stewart wasn't very welcoming, I hear,' Gabrielle said. 'Didn't he make some caustic remark?'

'Yes, but he had no business to, and having had that pointed out to him. . .by me, mind you. . .made a sort of apology, but not until afterwards. I shouldn't imagine he's the sort of man to find apologising very easy. He's far too sure of himself, as I'm sure you must have heard?

'Well, to get back to Andrew,' she remarked hastily, quelling Gabrielle with a slight frown, not wanting to talk about Iain just then, 'Andrew said, "And after all that, you had to face a gruelling interview! I'd have given up, had I been you."

'And I must say he looked pretty drained, almost as if he had been through Matthew's emergency with me!'

'There you are, he is sensitive and understanding!' Gabrielle took the chance to immediately spring to his defence.

'Maybe he is,' Mary smiled. 'Sorry for the criticism! Actually, at the time I did wonder myself whether it would be worth turning up for the interview, especially after the bad impression I must have given Consultant Stewart when I've openly differed from him at some regional casualty meetings. But I'm glad I conquered that defeatist feeling!'

And there she let the matter drop.

The next day brought a surprise invitation from Iain, one Mary found hard to resist. He phoned her at the Nightingale to say he had forgotten to tell her there was to be a senior staff barbecue in the grounds of a country house hotel that evening.

'But I'm not a member of the Glen's staff yet,' she pointed out.

'You almost are and it would be an opportunity for you to meet our consultants, nurse managers and administrators before you actually start work with us.'

True, thought Mary, knowing she would feel more at ease if at least slightly familiar with other seniors on the staff, so she agreed to accompany Iain who had offered also to provide transport.

'It depends on how the twins are, and whether I can get my friend Gabrielle to give Andrew a hand in looking after them for me,' she said however, adding as a proviso, 'and depending upon neither of them having another engagement for the evening, of course.'

Not that they wouldn't drop them like hot cakes

in order to be together in a home atmosphere for the few hours, she was thinking, knowing how well they were getting on together. . .not that she said anything of the sort to Iain.

'All right. If you don't ring me here in Casualty before five-thirty I'll take it you'll be coming,' he was saying—cutting her short as if not prepared to stay on the line to argue the point. 'Goodbye, now,' he added abruptly, ringing off.

Well, that wasn't very nice, thought Mary, who now found herself in two minds as to whether or not she would accompany him to the barbecue. It would be different, she said to herself, if he had taken the trouble to try and persuade me; then I might have obliged, sure he was keen to have me with him. But as she had to admit to herself, he had sounded as if he couldn't care less one way or the other.

Yet it wasn't as if she wanted him to want her with him. . .did she? Of course not, Mary shrugged, nevertheless finding herself hurrying along to ask Gabrielle whether she would be able to help Andrew look after the twins for an hour or so that evening.

'Phone Andrew and ask him if he's willing,' Gabrielle suggested with an unusual show of diffidence. 'I wouldn't like to ask him myself or he might think I'm after him.'

'Well?' Mary replied. 'Oh, sorry, I'm only teasing!' Then she phoned Andrew and came back with the news that he would be delighted to oblige, having wanted to stay in the flat that evening anyway, and wanted to know what

Gabrielle would like for supper as he was trying
to improve his culinary skills.

So the way was left clear for Mary to wait for
Iain to collect her.

She had not thought to ask at what time he
would come, so she played with her boys for a
while, bathed them, and read them a story as
usual after putting them to bed, then decided to
dress to kill, thinking of all the Royal Glen seniors
who would be meeting her for the first time.

She gave her twins a preview first, showing herself off in stylishly tailored white trousers topped
by the truly luxurious sweater she had not been
able to resist treating herself to when she saw it
in a sale reduced to half price.

The boys gazed at the appliquéd satin flower
garland crossing the ecru-coloured sweater to the
shoulder, and fingered the lustrous beading and
sequin detail with wonder in their eyes. 'You look
booful, Mummy,' Rob declared.

'Like a fairy princess,' agreed Richie.

So Mary gave them extra cuddles and tucked
them up saying she would wave a secret wand
over them to help them dream magic dreams, the
best coming to the one who fell asleep first.

Their blue eyes determinedly screwed up, Mary
crept out to the kitchen where she sat chatting to
Andrew and Gabrielle.

'I agree with Rob and Richie, you do look
"booful",' Andrew was just saying in a compli-
mentary tone after hearing what the twins had
said, when, at that very moment, Iain arrived. . .
so it was with heightened colour on her cheeks

that Mary went to open the door.

'You look better tonight,' Iain greeted her.

'Better than in Emergency RTA clothes?' Mary couldn't resist asking.

Not a muscle moved in Iain's face however. He merely greeted Gabrielle, nodded casually to Andrew, and promptly led Mary down to his car.

'That rig-out does more for you than RTA gear,' he acceded however as he walked with her down the cement steps.

'Thank you,' she bowed graciously although not thinking it much of a compliment. 'I'm out to make a good impression on all the high and mighty senior staff,' she explained demurely, trying to appear serious.

He gave her a shrewd look. 'From what I know of you already I don't think you'll ever bother to pander to any of them. . .'

'Not even to you?' she asked pertly.

'No, not even to me.' And he sighed as if he thought that a matter for regret, then, opening the car door for her and bending towards her as she sat down, he tucked a tartan travel rug over her knees before shutting the door. Mary, instantly reminded of Robert's unfailing courtesy towards her, felt a stab of pain in her heart, missing him more than ever.

'It's a nice evening so I thought we'd drive with the hood down,' Iain said, walking around to his driving seat. 'But would it mess up your hair, do you think?'

Drawn from her sad reverie, 'My hair has a will of its own,' Mary claimed despairingly. 'It does its own thing no matter how I try to subdue it!'

A funny sound came from Iain's throat which she thought could well have been his attempt to produce a laugh. He was truly a very sober sort of person, she decided, not at all like Robert, who had usually allowed his sense of humour full rein to help enliven any sad or weary company. . . such as hers at the moment.

Then Iain spoke, making her jerk up, she was so unprepared for him to bother. His question brought her back down to earth.

'What about this party of yours?' he was asking.

'Oh, I've decided to forget all about that,' she answered, quickly stopping herself from adding that he himself had killed the idea stone dead. 'Perhaps some other time in the future. . .' Her voice trailed away.

She was aware of him glancing her way as she gave her rather off-putting reply, but he made no attempt to pursue the subject, for which she was grateful, contenting herself with gazing around at the beautiful countryside instead, glorying in the open-air freedom, in the abundance of wild flowers blooming everywhere, the full-leafed trees in every shade of green, gracious tall and stately Scots pines, and the masses of pink and red and purple and white flowers edging the roadside, colours still gloriously visible although it was already evening.

'You're very quiet, not at all the bubbling vision I once saw skipping lively young twins along Beech Grove,' Iain remarked suddenly.

'You remember?' Mary was surprised, even

though every detail of that first outside-hospital encounter was still etched deeply into her own heart, she didn't quite know why.

'You seem to belong to the country,' Iain murmured. 'I should imagine you love it.'

'I do,' Mary said quietly. 'If I had my way I would live on the side of a mountain, woods all around me full of wild deer and frisky rabbits, with baby lambs playing against a background of golden gorse, unwinding fronds of ferns, tinkling waterfalls providing musical backgrounds. . .' she waxed enthusiastic. 'Oh, I would never tire of listening also to the song of birds, would watch waterfalls all day long if I could, pick fresh flowers to deck my pretty stone cottage—that's if I had one—grow my own food, happily surround myself with so much of the beauty and good things God created for our enjoyment. Ah, what sheer bliss a life like that could be!'

'With or without your boys?'

'Oh, they'd be an integral part of the whole idyllic scene,' Mary said dreamily.

Iain glanced towards her once or twice, a soft smile playing around his mouth as if he too were enjoying her quiet reverie. . .joining her in the picturesque scene she had conjured up.

'And would I be there too?' he asked, but so softly that she felt justified in pretending not to hear, just in case her voice betrayed the strange, sweet yearning she was beginning to experience.

CHAPTER EIGHT

UPON arrival at the site of the barbecue they found there were too many introductions and too much to see for personal conversations to be possible. It was only when Mary and Iain managed to break away that they had any time to themselves, and even then Mary was too tired to talk much, while as for Iain, he seemed totally absorbed in thought.

Eventually he broke the silence. 'You don't eat much,' he remarked, frowning. 'And when you do eat, it's such a slow process. Is there something wrong, Mary? Don't you enjoy eating?'

'I don't find it easy, to tell you the truth,' she answered. She paused, not really wanting to discuss herself. 'I'm sorry if I spoilt the barbecue for you by wanting to leave so soon,' she added, however.

'I only meant to stay an hour or so, anyway.' He walked her back to his car. 'And I knew you would want to get back to the boys as soon as possible. How is Rob, by the way?'

Mary's face brightened at the very thought of him. 'Fine!' she said enthusiastically. 'It is as though there's been nothing wrong with him at all. Mind you, I think we're spoiling him, and spoiling Richie too so that he won't feel neglected in favour of Rob!'

Iain still seemed unduly concerned, looking at

Mary discerningly and asking her how much weight she had lost in the last few months, although when she admitted to being less than seven and a half stone instead of the eight and a half she had been previously, he tactfully changed the subject, able to see for himself that she was beginning to feel awkward being questioned about herself.

'Young Matthew is in a paediatric ward now, no longer in Intensive Care,' he said unexpectedly. 'His folk are looking forward to you visiting him with them as they say you promised.'

'I didn't actually promise,' Mary corrected, 'at least I don't think so, but I did intend to try to visit him with them. The trouble is I've been so busy I quite forgot.' She looked genuinely ashamed of her lapse of memory. 'There are so many patients coming and going, it's hard to keep track of them all, no matter how much one intends to or wants to,' she said by way of excuse.

'I know,' Iain agreed. 'But if you do want to see Matthew, what about lunchtime tomorrow—could you get away?'

'We're very short-staffed, but I'll try.'

She still sounded flustered and added, 'I should be working in your A and E department in a week or so, when it would be much easier for me to visit him. Couldn't I leave it until then? I've so much to do, and so little time in which to do it. That's what made me apply for the staff-grade job, after all. I wanted more time to myself.'

She could have bitten the words back as soon as she had said them, and sure enough Iain frowned.

'Which wasn't the best of reasons,' he grunted. 'I was beginning to believe you had a more idealistic aim. So you are prepared to disappoint Matthew after all he has been through? He and his family are gathering at his bedside tomorrow expecting you to be with them as they were told.'

Mary jerked back at his words. 'Who told them—you? Well, you had no right to do so!' she declared angrily.

Rebuked, Iain looked annoyed. He stopped the car and they stared at one another, friction in the air. Then, 'We're short-staffed too,' Iain pointed out. 'You'll be kept fully occupied all day long in my department, I can promise you.'

'Not all day long,' Mary answered back, 'I think you're already forgetting I'll be staff-grade, working a forty-hour week, not a hundred plus as up to now.'

He mellowed. 'Anyway, do come tomorrow; I'll stand you a lunch in our canteen. It's a bigger one than yours.'

'Bigger lunch or bigger canteen?' she couldn't resist asking, weary as she was.

'Can't miss quipping, can you, Mary, Mary, quite contrary?' he said ironically, then, surprising her, laid a hand over hers, drawing it on to the gear lever to rest under his strong warm fingers.

Mary's heart lurched and she quickly drew her hand away. But what worried her when she thought about the incident afterwards was the instant thrill she had experienced at his touch.

He parked the car outside her flat. His face

was grave. He opened her car door for her then stood back.

'See you tomorrow then, twelve-thirty,' he said as she got out and ran up the concrete steps. 'Do come, Mary, there's something important I want to talk to you about.'

'Goodnight.' Her voice was soft and subdued. 'I'll try,' she said.

He watched her go into the porch, but she made no attempt to look back.

Slowly he slid into the driving seat of his car, while Mary, for her part, crept silently into the darkness of the tiny front lounge to steal a quiet, thoughtful moment to herself, needing to calm her disturbed feelings down before having to face Andrew and Gabrielle and any questions they might ask, purposely taking time to herself to wonder what it was Iain was wanting to say to her.

Meeting him the next lunchtime as arranged, she waited for him to start talking, growing increasingly apprehensive when he seemed to have difficulty in beginning to put whatever it was into words, even in the canteen waiting to be served, Mary staying with him to make her own selection of the dishes on offer.

Stunned by her choice of a meagre helping of cauliflower cheese, he eyed it with concern. 'Is that all you're having?' he asked in something like alarm, roast chicken, stuffing, sausage and bacon rolls, duchesse potatoes and sprouts almost over-loading his own plate.

'It's enough,' Mary replied.

With an earnest and rather worried expression

he sat down facing her across the small table for two he had selected in an almost hidden alcove.

'I'm worried about you,' he began after salting his dinner. 'Worried about you and the small amount you're eating. It's hardly enough to keep a fly alive! Not only that, but the amount seems to get smaller each day! *Is* there something wrong, Mary? That's what I want to know. . .'

'Why should there be?' The last thing Mary had thought him wanting to discuss was her appetite, or rather the lack of it.

'You can't go on like this; you're already losing weight much too rapidly!' he remonstrated quite crossly.

Trying to take no notice, she continued toying with her food, eating nothing, then said, very quietly, feeling he was sincere in his concern on her behalf, 'Will it make you any happier about me if I tell you it isn't that I've gone off food, it is just that I really and truly don't seem able to swallow it properly? It sticks about halfway down, making me very uncomfortable. I need constant drinks to help move it, not that they always help.'

She kept her eyes downcast, not knowing how he would take her explanation, but her relief in at last explaining her difficulty was almost overwhelming, especially as she was now so aware that her problems were getting worse. She knew too that like many of her patients, she had been dodging having to face up to the fact that there was something wrong with her that needed treatment, and her temper was suffering as a result.

'I didn't want anyone to know,' she continued

without glancing up at Iain, 'because I was scared it might go against me at the interview, but now that I've realised how abrupt I am with you, how I tend to snap at my twins even when they don't deserve it, and——' her voice dropped '—even good friends like Gabrielle and Andrew are tending to avoid me, being uncomfortable in my presence. . .well, I know I've got to do something to remedy matters.'

'You suffer pain?' Iain asked caringly.

'I did, night after night, and during the day sometimes, but now that's easing off a bit, although the swallowing difficulty is getting worse and I wake up at night choking, although if I prop myself up in bed with cushions piled behind me that does seem to help.' Mary had to fight against an attack of self-pity, tears very near again. . .

'Your parents are in Germany, I know,' Iain interrupted her thinking, 'but couldn't your mother come over to help you?'

Mary shook her head. 'I've no intention of asking her,' she said stubbornly. 'She has her own problems, rheumatoid arthritis being only one of many.'

Then, seeing the solicitude in Iain's eyes, for the first time she felt really grateful for his attempted understanding, realising he was the only person to whom she could turn in her present predicament.

'What I was thinking,' he began, purposely looking away from her, as if not wanting to cause her more embarrassment, 'or what I was hoping really, is that you would allow a colleague of mine to have a look at you. He is known to be a brilliant gastroenterologist and might be able to help. At least he could give you tests to determine exactly what is happening.'

'Tests? What for?' Mary looked up, fear shadowing her eyes and what little colour she had already draining from her cheeks. 'I can't afford to have anything wrong with me,' she almost pleaded, then, remembering Iain's prejudice against working mothers, she was careful not to express her fear of having to spend any time away from her sons, so changed what she had been about to say to ask instead when his colleague would be likely to see her.

'In his next outpatients' clinic, I imagine.' Iain spoke nonchalantly and she wondered whether that was on purpose to quieten her fears. He was very astute and would surely have guessed at her feelings in the matter.

Debbie-Ann will be back from South Africa soon, and Andrew will be starting work in Orthopaedics, she mused, beginning to think that if there was something that needed sorting out, perhaps it might be as well to get the treatment started soon rather than later. After all, she knew that if an operation was needed she would have to go on to the waiting list just like anyone else, so the boys would probably be in kindergarten by that time and that would might make things easier all round.

'I can almost hear your mind buzzing!' Iain said, interrupting her thoughts.

'It's because I think I know what my trouble is.' Mary decided to be honest with him. 'I haven't

wanted to face up to having achalasia, but in my
heart I have known all along that that's probably
what it is. Besides—' she smiled wryly '—I looked
it up in my *Oxford Textbook of Medicine*.'

'Then wished you hadn't, I expect?' Iain
sounded so empathetic that she was glad she no
longer had to keep her secret to herself.

'What puzzles me,' she added, 'is that according
to the book I'm rather young to have achalasia.'

'I would have thought so too, but considering
the preceding years of over-long working hours,
disrupted mealtimes and extreme exhaustion such
as most young doctors experience, added to the
trauma of losing your husband, it's not to be wondered at if the symptoms of achalasia showed
themselves earlier than normal. Rob's developing
meningitis couldn't have helped you, either!'

Appreciating his unexpected understanding and
obvious sympathy, Mary found her eyes moisten-
ing and stood up, anxious to leave the canteen
before the floodgates could open. She had been
worrying day and night, knowing how ill she was
beginning to feel.

Now, having someone share her secret and
growing anxiety—even if that someone had to
be Iain—brought such an overwhelming sense of
relief that all Mary wanted at that moment was
to go away by herself and have a good cry. Tears
never seemed far away these days, she thought
wistfully.

As if sensitive to her feelings, Iain handed her
the large clean handkerchief from his white coat's
top pocket. For a moment she buried her face

in it, surreptitiously wiping her tears away, then, controlling her emotions, she came up smiling again.

'I'm sorry,' she said.

Iain waved her tentative apology away.

'It's time for us both to get back to work,' he remarked gently, 'but before I go there's one other thing I'd like to mention. I'll have to be quick about it.'

'Oh?' Mary wondered what was coming next.

'It's about your boys. They lack a proper place to play out of doors, as I'm sure you agree. Keen footballers they certainly are, but having to prac- tise on the gravel outside your flat isn't doing their knees any good; they're forever cut and bruised, aren't they? Well, I have a proposition to make. I know where they could play on grass to their hearts' content. . .and in safety, what's more.'

'You do?' Her eyes opened wide again.

'Well, you might not know it, but beyond those ornamental gates you once tried to make me believe were yours——' his mouth curved into one of his rare smiles '—lies my family home, grandparents, my niece and her nanny living there with a small staff. That's how I knew it was not your home too.'

Mary's cheeks pinkened guiltily.

'Don't worry.' He gave her fingers a little understanding squeeze before she could move them out of his reach. 'I share your sort of pride, am a bit of a rebel too in my way, preferring independence even from those I love, which is why I chose to live in the little Gate House you might have noticed on the left-hand side of the drive.'

Mary felt uncomfortable, remembering how the twins had peered through the gates.

'Anyway, what I'm meaning to say,' Iain went on, 'is that if you do have to go into hospital as a patient, my family and my niece's nanny would be only too happy to care for the twins; in fact, they actually hanker to have more children around.'

'Perhaps you're only presupposing that?'

His face sobered. 'No, I don't think so. I'm sure you would be doing them a good turn; in fact——' He hesitated, to continue a little reservedly, 'I can't tell you here and now, but there's quite a tragic story to lend weight to my belief. . . Listen, I'll be finished at eight; let's go for a short drive then and I'll explain further.

'I've got to get back to work now.' He pushed his chair back and stood up. 'Come and I'll give you a lift to your Nightingale, but we'll have to hurry. So what about tonight?'

Accompanying Iain to his car, Mary, her curiosity aroused, agreed to the evening drive with the proviso that she would be able to make arrangements to leave the children in good hands.

'Regarding your offer to allow the twins to play in the grounds of your house, thank you. I'll give it a lot of thought,' she said quietly before getting into the car, then suddenly stopped in her tracks. 'Oh, I've been forgetting all about seeing Matthew,' she gasped, turning back, quite horrified at her lapse of memory.

'Come to him now,' Iain urged, reaching out and catching hold of her arm. 'There's still time if we hurry.' Then, seeing Andrew leaving his borrowed car and coming towards them, he dropped Mary's arm quite abruptly.

'You wanted us?' he greeted Andrew.

'Not really.' Andrew looked awkward. 'I rather wanted to be shown the whole of the Glen's orthopaedic unit,' he muttered, 'but intended giving Mary a lift back to Nightingale's Casualty first. I've time to spare before collecting the twins from playschool.'

'Was it Gabrielle you wanted to see, or me?' Mary teased, more for Iain's benefit than for Andrew's, hoping that by implying that Andrew was as keen on Gabrielle as on her she would lessen the chance of further animosity growing between the two men.

'Excuse us.' Iain appeared in a hurry to leave nevertheless. 'Otherwise we'll be too late to keep our appointments,' he said rather brusquely to Andrew. 'Ask for Dr Gardner in Orthopaedics; he's an obliging sort of chap and will make a good job of showing you the ropes up there. . .'

'And wait for me afterwards, Andrew, if I'm not already out by your friend's vehicle,' Mary said with an appealing smile. 'I'm due back on duty in fifteen minutes so I shan't keep you waiting.'

'And my offer of a lift is turned down in his favour?' Iain remarked a little sourly as together he and Mary walked into Matthew's ward.

'I knew you had work to do, whereas he hasn't,'

Mary said placatingly. Then, catching sight of
Matthew and his family, she hurried along to
them, Iain with her to give them a short greeting,
then leaving to go to his own department.

'I'm sorry we were late getting here,' apologised
Matthew's mother when Mary joined her, 'but
there was some sort of hold-up with the buses.'

'That's quite all right,' Mary smiled, going to
Matthew's bedside and holding his hand, relieved
to know she had not kept the little family waiting.
Then asking Matthew how he felt now, she chat-
ted to the happy little group and joked with him,
delighted to see how well he had progressed.

'We don't often see our patients after helping
to pull them round after accidents,' she explained
to his family. 'This is a rare treat for me. Usually
we're too busy with the next casualties to be able
to do more than pass on those to whom we have
given the necessary immediate help—leaving
them in the care of the doctors and surgeons
skilled in the follow-up treatment such as operations.'

'I hadn't thought of that,' said Matthew's
mother. 'I hope we're not holding you back from
seeing to someone else right now?'

'Well, I do have to hurry——' through the
window Mary had caught a glimpse of Andrew
walking to the car '—but it has been lovely seeing
you all, especially with Matthew looking so bright
and cheerful.' And, bidding the family farewell,
she left, waving from the doorway before she disappeared into the corridor to join up with Andrew
outside.

After arriving at the Nightingale Mary left Andrew talking to Gabrielle while she busied herself with the special patients the nurses had kept back for her to see to, a usual practice of theirs in cases when they felt the new and inexperienced doctors would not be able to give the help she could.

It was not until it was time for her to go off duty that she had a chance to speak to Gabrielle, and when she did, the two of them slipping into the canteen for a quick cup of coffee, Gabrielle quite shocked Mary by coming out with a complaint about Andrew. 'What's wrong with him, do you know?' she asked.

'Wrong with him?' Mary echoed. 'Nothing. Why should there be?'

'He came in very disgruntled, not at all like his old self. Was very short with me.'

Mary thought back, realising that he had hardly said a word to her either—well, not since seeing Iain holding her arm. Surely, she thought, that could not have affected him in any way? No, not Andrew!

'He was OK with me,' she said unthinkingly.

'But not with me, which shows he prefers you.'

'This is too much!' Already overwrought after the trying events of the day, Mary slammed her cup back on to its saucer. 'I don't want to be drawn into any controversy of this sort. I thought I had made it crystal-clear to everyone that when Robert died he took my heart with him. If any man wants to flatter his own ego by presuming I'd be interested in him in the romantic sense, he needs his head seeing to! I am sure Andrew realises that as much as anyone, so whatever gave you the impression that he prefers me must exist only in your own imagination, Gabrielle.'

'I didn't mean to upset you,' Gabrielle said abjectly.

'Well, truth to tell I've had just about enough of sly innuendoes and suggestions coming at me from all directions, people refusing to believe that my memories of the great happiness I knew with Robert would suffice to content me for the rest of my life. They presume I must need something more. I ask you! Who can be the judge of that? No one except me!'

'I *have* upset you—me and my big mouth!' exclaimed Gabrielle. 'It was mean of me to say anything.'

'Don't regret it. . .you've given me the chance to blow my top,' Mary said with a wry smile, 'so, taking a tip from TV's *Mastermind* programme, "I've started, so I'll finish". . . What's happening is completely crazy: Andrew is sometimes jealous of Iain Stewart, Iain is vexed by Andrew, you're afraid I might be taking Andrew away from you, Debbie-Ann might well think me trying to attract him from *her*, and here am I, the innocent party in all this and not able to defend myself because no one will believe I am just not interested in any males except Rob and Richie. . .and my father, of course.'

Mary laughed, but there was no real mirth in her laughter. 'I don't want Iain, I don't want Andrew, I just want Robert and I can't have him, that's the tragedy of it. I could never love anyone else in the way I loved him, and still love him. Losing him was like losing half of myself, and that's the truth.'

She put out a hand to Gabrielle, 'Now, let's not discuss it any more. Come home with me, and you, Andrew, the boys and I will have tea together.'

CHAPTER NINE

HOWEVER, the next day the conflict widened, Gabrielle remarking—albeit peacefully—that Andrew still wasn't his old cheerful self and that she now knew why.

'It's because of Iain Stewart,' she declared.

'Do you think Andrew will be better once he starts work?' Mary asked. 'Perhaps he needs to be more fully occupied?'

'Well certainly he can't have much fun with only five pounds a week in his pocket.'

Mary sighed. 'I can't afford to give him more. I still have Debbie to pay; she'll be hard-up after paying her return fare. I must help her with it.'

'I know that, and so does Andrew; the problem is that he sees Iain able to take you about and spend money on you.'

'Which hasn't happened very often,' Mary reminded her.

'Often enough to annoy Andrew.'

'Why, has he actually said so?'

'Not in so many words but one would have to be pretty obtuse not to realise how he is feeling, and thinking. . .'

'But he hasn't actually said anything? That's strange; I would have thought he'd have complained to you, if not to anyone else, you get on so well; at least, you did. . .'

Gabrielle pulled a wry face. 'We would have got on better had he not met you first.'

'Oh, no, don't let's start that again,' Mary sighed. 'Let's just get on with our jobs. All I personally want is to do my work well, help people as best I can, avoid getting entangled in any love triangle and be left in peace to bring up my twins in my own way.'

With a hangdog look, Gabrielle muttered, 'Point taken,' then, a moment later, when with cheeks dimpling Mary gave her one of her encouraging smiles, she relaxed. 'I haven't been helping you much, have I?' she said, adding a very sincere, 'But, you know something, Mary. . .in spite of the suffering you must endure, I think you are very lucky to have experienced a love such as you and Robert shared.'

Her words brought solace on what had been a particularly trying day for Mary.

Some of the so-called 'regulars'—or 'gentlemen of the road' as they were referred to sometimes, had come into Casualty to shelter from the heavy rain, and one or two had even tried to snatch a nap on trolleys, from where it had been hard work persuading them to dislodge themselves. Mary alone seemed to have the knack of dealing with the men in a way they would accept.

'She talks to us like we're fellow human beings,' one was heard to say appreciatively.

'Well, they are, aren't they?' Mary declared defiantly when someone then argued against her charitable attitude. 'Just folk who've fallen on bad times and not known how to cope. If the pressures were heavy enough I suppose it could happen to any of us. Without knowledge of their background or excuses, we're in no position to judge them.'

Then she went along to help one fight his battle against emphysema, an obstructive airways disease, his breathlessnes and wheezing 'scaring him stiff', he said, so she had a job on her hands trying to calm him down while at the same time treating his condition.

After which a lady was brought in, her ankle injured. Another case the nurses wanted Mary to deal with herself. It was a lighter moment, however, for although in pain from the ankle, the lady enlivened the department with her sense of humour, she made so much of the fact that the cause of her accident was a simple little grape!

'I slipped on it in the supermarket,' she chuckled. 'You never saw such a furore! Assistants appearing as if from nowhere, running here, running there, shoppers standing gaping, or edging away thinking I'd been attacked and becoming wary for their own safety, two big men and one frail little lady trying to help me to my feet only to find I couldn't stand!'

She chuckled before continuing, 'I thought for a moment that they were going to pile me into a shopping trolley and wheel me away! Then the store manager arrived, all apologies and with two girl assistants following him carrying a non-slip rug as if it were his train and laying it before the boxes of grapes. . .which was rather like locking the stable door after the horse had bolted, I thought.

'Anyway, an ambulance was sent for and with curious people gathering in the store and around outside like a Guard of Honour, I was driven away ready to wave back in the regal manner, only the windows were too dark to enable me to be seen. . .such a pity!'

Mary finished examining the ankle. 'We'll get it X-rayed,' she said, 'but I don't think it's broken. Sprained, more likely.'

'After all that fuss!' the patient exclaimed humorously. 'Now I don't know whether I'll ever have the nerve to show my face inside that supermarket again!'

'Or show your ankle?' Mary laughed, calling for the still necessary wheelchair transport, then turning to see to a young girl who had had her head butted by a horse.

'Do you think it broke her nose?' the eleven-year-old's mother asked anxiously.

'I'll make sure she hasn't septal haematoma. . . blood swelling of the septum,' Mary explained to the mother, then recommended the young girl not to blow her nose, but to be 'thoroughly unsociable' and keep sniffing instead!

She turned again to the girl's mother. 'Until the swelling lessens it's hard to see whether or not the nose is broken,' she told her, 'but if it looks crooked in a week's time when the swelling's gone down, take your daughter to your GP who will then refer her to the ear, nose and throat department. If necessary, the nose can be straightened under the NHS. All right?'

She patted the young girl on the shoulder. 'And

remember, no blowing, only gentle sniffing,' she reminded her quietly.

Then, her duties over for the day, Mary allowed herself to remember that from the next Monday onwards she would be actually working with Iain Stewart. It was a sobering thought!

'I'll have to try to make a good impression some time,' she decided, wondering if the arranged evening drive would provide a suitable opportunity.

But when, having to take over from Andrew that day she managed to arrange to leave her hospital in time to collect the twins from their playgroup, she received an unpleasant shock. The group leader asked for a private word with her and when they were alone looked awkward, then—as if forcing herself—told her of a rumour her boys had originated.

'Rumour?' Mary frowned, puzzled. 'Why, what on earth could they have said?'

'Only that they have two fathers, one for nights, and another for during daytimes!' The playgroup leader stiffened disapprovingly, but Mary had a job to curb her laughter, thinking the rumour the funniest thing she had heard in a long time.

However, she was obviously meant to take the matter seriously, judging from the expression on the other young woman's face.

'Some of the mothers are looking askance at the twins now, probably wondering if they will have a bad influence on their own little ones; in fact several have already expressed concern,' she was continuing.

Mary could hardly believe what she was hearing. 'They can't mean it, surely?' she gasped.

'Some people have a very "holier than thou" attitude, I'm afraid.'

'But every parent knows that young children often get hold of the wrong end of the stick, not really realising the significance of what they're saying,' Mary argued defensively.

'Nevertheless people believe what they want to believe, and everyone loves a bit of scandal. I thought you ought to know what is being said.' The playgroup leader's manner hardened.

Mary nodded. 'Yes. Thank you for telling me. I can see why the boys said what they did. Dr Andrew Buchan—well, he's a Mr Buchan really because, like me, he has his Fellowship of the Royal College of Surgeons——' she was deliberately trying to add an imposing air of respectability to them both '—has been given an appointment as orthopaedic registrar in the Royal Glen hospital starting on August the first, when he will move into hospital accommodation. In the meantime he has nowhere to live, and because Debbie-Ann, my childminder, is visiting her sick father in Cape Town, he is taking her place in looking after the twins while I'm at work.'

'And lives with you meanwhile?'

'Sleeps in Debbie-Ann's room while she's away,' Mary stated forcefully, beginning to grow angry at the insinuations.

'And the other man the boys mention?'

'Is the consultant of the casualty department I shall be working in from August the first, and which is also in the Royal Glen hospital. He would be very vexed if he thought anyone was linking us in any romantic sense. I would be angry too. He was good to Rob when he had meningitis and still likes to keep an eye on him, and that is *all*!'

Mary spoke firmly, hoping she had said enough to scotch the upsetting rumour, although judging from the other young woman's pursed lips she had not been too successful.

'Is Mr Buchan a trained childminder?' the group-leader was asking disapprovingly a moment's thought later. 'If not, he has no right to be doing the job!'

Mary could have told her that Debbie-Ann had no right, either. Although she was a fully trained nanny in South Africa, her qualifications were not recognised in Great Britain. She kept quiet about that, however, glad her twins would be transferring to kindergarten soon, hopefully before trouble could be raised about Debbie-Ann.

Her badly dented sense of humour and fun were however rejuvenated by the sight of Rob and Richie rushing to give her a welcoming hug and almost falling over each other in their excitement at seeing her.

In happy response she allowed them full rein on the playground equipment in the park until they tired themselves out, then walked them back to the flat, still saddened yet bemused by the idea of them thinking they had two fathers.

She knew she would have some explaining to do, but how much would they understand; when would they be able to realise that a third man. . .

her beloved Robert, was their one and only real 'dad'?

At the moment, she thought, he was nothing more to them than a cherished photograph on the mantelpiece, no matter how hard she tried to make him appear vividly alive to their minds and hearts.

However, when actually back in the flat and, worn out by all their activity in the park, the twins had tea then were content to play quietly with their toys, Mary was able to relax with time to think, and found herself viewing the ill-founded rumour from a different and more worrying angle.

What could she do about it? she wondered. If becoming more widespread it could easily damage Iain's reputation, to say nothing of hers and Andrew's! Definitely that could not be allowed to happen. Could not and should not be allowed. But—how to prevent it?

It was an intriguing situation but not one she welcomed. She was still debating whether or not to keep the disquieting news to herself when Andrew and Gabrielle arrived to help with the boys and all chance of a quiet chat with them to tell them what had happened was lost in the ensuing noise and confusion of the bedtime bath and bed routine.

Then, no sooner were the children in bed than Iain was at the front door ready to take her out.

They drove for quite a few minutes before he started to speak, and, even his profile expressing deep sorrow, with a break in his voice, he told her about the horrific plane accident in which his parents, sister and brother-in-law had lost their lives.

Cautiously he had slowed down his driving as he spoke, then, obviously still inwardly grieving for them, he parked in a lay-by and waited a moment or two before continuing his sad tale.

'Fortunately Emma, my little niece, my sister's daughter, had not accompanied her parents. Being a mere baby at the time, she had remained at home with her nanny and great-grandparents.

'The set-up remains the same,' he continued, 'except that I moved down from a hospital in Aberdeen to the Royal Glen especially to be near them. I've been here ever since but I don't remember coming in *real* contact with you until recently.' He gazed at her, a semblance of an engaging smile replacing his sad look.

'I've been working and studying hard,' Mary remarked, perking up because he had suddenly brightened. 'Only joined the Nightingale about a year ago, then my father was posted to Germany and Mother went with him, but not before she had found me a good childminder she was confident would supply the necessary help with the twins. Help she herself had been giving me since their birth.'

'That's where your Debbie-Ann came in, I suppose?'

'Yes, she answered an advertisement in the paper and we liked the sound of her. There was no answer that even compared with hers. Besides,' Mary smiled, 'she comes from Cape

Town, where my mother was born, which was an added enticement!'

'Has your childminder ever mentioned three-year-old Emma, my niece, or her nanny?' Iain asked. 'I should think they must have met sometimes when toing or froing from the playschool?'

Mary thought for a moment then returned a blank look. 'Not that I recall,' she said.

'Emma's a quiet little thing, I think she needs bringing out of herself,' Iain remarked thoughtfully. 'That's a way in which your boys could help. From what I've seen of them so far, they might well be just the sort of company she needs.'

'You want to turn her into a tomboy?' Mary looked amused.

'No, just into a girl who can stand up for herself.' Iain was still being serious. 'The sort of girl you are, for instance. . .'

'Oh, you see me like that, do you?' she remarked, surprised. 'Well, I'll gave the matter some thought.' She paused, a frown puckering her brow. 'But I didn't have any brothers,' she stated.

'Which was probably just as well.' Iain half laughed, but made no attempt to explain what he meant. He did start up the car again, however and continue with the drive, although not for long. He parked in the next lay-by, one sheltered by large, bushy trees.

'You know, Mary,' he began reflectively, 'somewhere right inside you there are turbulent waters trying to stir up your emotions, but sadly you have layered them with a stillness they can't

break through. I long to disturb that surface of
stillness and delve down into the depths that lie
at the very heart of you. I presume Robert was
able to get through?'

'That's another question you shouldn't ask.'
Mary blinked rapidly to clear the moisture threatening to cloud her eyes. 'What Robert was to me,
and I to him, is nobody's business but ours. People
are forever trying to probe. I find it most
upsetting.'

'I'm sorry.' Iain's arm went around her and she
allowed it to stay, finding comfort in his hold as
before, besides not wanting him to feel rejected,
she didn't quite know why.

'All I know is that you are beginning to get
into my system,' Iain was saying seriously, his arm
moving to her shoulder, his fingers resting lightly
against her neck, reminding her of his touch in
the canteen when he had passed behind her. As
on that day, she found herself trembling.

'Don't shrink from me, Mary,' he urged. 'I want
to feel the nearness of you, to know the comfort
I am sure you could give if only you would allow
yourself. . .don't banish natural feelings of tenderness, affection, or love itself, or you'll grow
hard. You are too locked up inside. . .'

Her answer was nothing more than a sob, an
almost silent sob.

He turned her face towards him. 'Do you feel
all right, or are you in pain?' he asked solicitously.
'Look here, Mary, you'll have to let me make
arrangements for my friend to see you in clinic.
Have I your permission to do so?'

She simply nodded her agreement to have her symptoms of achalasia investigated, and from his deep sigh of relief knew how anxious he was about her condition.

'Good girl!' he exclaimed in approval. 'And when you have had yourself sorted out I think perhaps you should get married again.' He spoke quietly and gently.

Nevertheless, 'Get married again?' Mary repeated indignantly, thrusting him away from her. 'I thought you understood how I felt about Robert,' she snapped, her chin quivering. 'You can't realise what you're saying! Get married again? How could you even suggest such a thing?'

'Someone has to, Mary, you can't continue to go through life on your own. Oh, I know you have the boys, but the day will come when they will make lives of their own, marry, have families. . .and you might be left alone. You are much too young and—dare I say it—too attractive and spirited to go through the rest of your life without a partner. There must be many a man who would treasure a wife like you.'

Mary noticed that he did not include himself. Not that she wanted him to, she reminded herself. All the same, she was missing the comfort of his arm and wishing she had not been in such a hurry to disengage herself from it.

See the influence he's trying to exert over me, she half-sobbed inside, growing more perturbed by the minute as she went over and over his words in her mind. He wants me to forget my feelings for Robert, to give my love to someone else instead! He has no understanding, no knowledge of real feelings, that much is evident. I was wrong in presuming he had!

'You're a fine one to talk of remarrying,' she declared frostily. 'You've never married at all, have you, or so I'm told?'

'I take it you've been enquiring?' He smiled teasingly. 'No, I've never married. I'm particular, have never found the girl I'd want to live my life with. . .well, not until. . .' He failed to finish the sentence.

'I would like to go home now.' Mary turned away from him, although, 'Yes, I will let the gastroenterologist test me for achalasia,' she agreed quietly if also rather unwillingly, 'but only because it is manifestly the most sensible thing to do, especially as I have the twins to keep fit for. But I warn you, I shall reject any interference in my private life. Get married again? The very idea. . . Huh! You obviously don't know what it is to love, really love someone. But *I* do.'

After a slight pause she went on dreamily, 'I know how the sun can shine on a cloudy day just because of a smile, I've experienced the rapture that can grow from a kiss, the comfort, even thrill, of a touch from a special well-loved hand, and have learnt that nothing can ever replace the warmth of a greeting from the lips of the one who means more to you than life itself. Such a wonderful all-embracing love can mount to sheer ecstasy and never falter or be replaced. Even when death intervenes nothing really alters, feelings stay the same.'

Iain studied her face, seeing the faraway look in her blue eyes as she continued softly, almost as if speaking to herself, 'Love, real love, remains in the heart, stronger and more passionate than ever before because protected. No harsh words, no unkindness, nothing bad is able to mar or spoil it, guarded as it is by the one to whom you so willingly gave it, and who keeps it safe for all eternity where all true hearts belong.

'I'm just not able to express my feelings adequately, but do you understand what I mean?' It was as if Mary were imploring him to try. 'I have to guard against being disloyal to Robert or I wouldn't be able to live with myself.' The face she turned away from Iain wore a tortured expression.

'Robert was a very lucky man,' Iain muttered as once before, but so quietly that Mary could scarcely distinguish his words. Near to tears again, she kept her gaze firmly fixed on the passing moonlit scenery as he drove her back to her flat.

'About your twins—what do you think of the idea I suggested in that direction?' He still seemed subdued as they parted by her front steps. 'Will you let them come and play in our grounds, always under the supervision of Emma's nanny, of course, my grandparents being in their eighties and not all that agile?' He tried to sound light-hearted, but was not altogether successful.

'I don't know,' she replied, her eyes downcast, 'I'll have to think about it.' Then she remembered what the leader of the playgroup had said and wondered whether her twins would be welcomed at the big house if the worrying rumour reached there.

Which, she knew, it was more than likely to do, especially as Iain's niece attended the same playschool as the twins.

'Do you know a three-year-old called Emma?' was the first thing she asked Andrew when she went indoors after leaving Iain. 'She goes to the twins' playschool and has a nanny who probably takes her there and back.'

Andrew thought for a moment then, 'Yes, I know them,' he said finally, 'but we only meet occasionally. Why?'

'What is the nanny like?' Mary asked.

'Too old for me,' Andrew grimaced. 'Why, are you trying to find me a soulmate?'

'Does she seem nice? That's what I want to know.'

'Too nice for me!' Andrew quipped.

'Don't be silly, I'm being serious!'

'All right,' Andrew sobered. 'She seems pleasant enough, that's all I can tell you about her.'

'And little Emma, what is she like?'

'Not a child to attract much notice. Shy, intro-verted perhaps, quite clever for her age I should think. Why, what's all this in aid of?'

'Nothing.' Mary tossed her head. 'What's for supper, have you had any?' she asked, changing the subject.

'No, I was waiting for you,' said Andrew. 'How would you fancy sardines on toast?'

'At this time of night? No, thank you! I think I'll go straight to bed.'

And do some thinking about my latest problem, Mary could have added, but she didn't. Not for anything in the world would she want Andrew to tease her about Iain, as well he might!

Iain was becoming quite a problem, in more ways than one!

CHAPTER TEN

MARY faced one of the biggest challenges of her life when she walked through the entrance doors of the Royal Glen's Accident and Emergency department to start work there.

She knew some of the nurses, having met them either at inter-hospital social functions, or on the wards when Rob was a patient, but it was the day for the big six-monthly influx of new SHOs who were stepping up after doing a year as housemen, most of them as yet undecided about which branch of medicine they would eventually choose to specialise in.

She had not met any of the new doctors before so found herself very interested in getting to know them, especially as she was supposed to teach them the ins and outs of Casualty workings.

There was no sign of Iain at first, but when he did come in he walked straight up to her.

Her heart quickened. What was he going to say? she wondered. After her outburst of the evening before, how was he feeling towards her? She stole a look at his face. It was very solemn.

He bent towards her, then in a low voice said only, 'I've made an appointment for you; my friend will see you at two o'clock.' And with that he strode away into his office.

Which left her nonplussed as to what to do

next, but fortunately an SHO came to her to ask
her advice regarding an X-ray he was holding,
and she was soon absorbed in explaining her find-
ings and in instructing him as to the treatment
the patient would need.

True to her earlier resolve, she was not wearing
a white coat, but the badge printed especially for
her plainly stated she was 'Mrs Mary Macgregor,
Casualty Team, Staff-grade Doctor'. However, as
some of the patients she saw in clinic that morning
either disregarded or were unable to read the
badge, and instead openly questioned what she
did and just who she was, some thinking her a
nurse and one in particular demanding to see 'a
proper doctor' when puzzled by her lack of any
sort of uniform, she took care to introduce herself
fully to all and sundry from then on.

When she did get time to think, she realised
she had no idea of the name of the medical special-
ist she was supposed to see, so, taking her courage
in both hands, she sought out Iain and found him
having a coffee in the department's kitchen.

'His name?' he said when she asked him.
'George McBrayne. He's the gastroenterologist.
Are you wanting a coffee? Here, I'll pour you
one. And Mary, have you thought any more about
my idea regarding your boys?'

'Not really,' she replied, refusing the coffee, but
appreciating his obvious attempt to let bygones be
bygones. 'My mind has been more occupied with
my change of job than anything,' she said, 'and
tonight Debbie-Ann is due back, so Andrew will
be moving out of her room and into the flat he's

been awaiting in the doctors' accommodation block over here.'

She purposely added that last piece of information, anxious to let him know that Andrew had not been permanently installed in her place in case he too had heard the rumour being spread abroad about her twins claiming to have two fathers.

What he would think if he also heard that *he* was suspected of being their second or third 'dad' she dreaded to think, so with the whole matter very much on her mind she made some excuse to hurry away from the coffee-room.

She saw George McBrayne at exactly two o'clock. He, like Iain, was very sharp and businesslike about his work, and after questioning her about her symptoms said he would arrange for her to have a barium meal X-ray and motility studies, then gave her an X-ray card to take down to that department, marking it 'member of staff'.

That done, he rose from behind his desk and in a much more friendly and relaxed way said he would walk her down to the investigations unit to arrange motility studies for the coming Wednesday, adding that he would see her again on the following Monday when he should be in possession of all the results.

'After that?' Mary asked, trying not to appear over-anxious.

'If it's achalasia you'll see the upper-gastrointestinal surgeon in his outpatients' suite and we'll go from there. Probably there'll be a balloon dilatation, but as a surgeon yourself you will know all about that?' He smiled at her.

'I've seen a few,' Mary replied, then, purposely making light of the matter although inwardly far from happy, 'but it's not a thing one can do on oneself,' she added.

He laughed, then seeing Iain coming along the corridor behind them, waited for him to catch up.

'Can I have my new staff-grade doctor back now?' Iain asked peremptorily.

'I didn't think you'd let her go for long,' George taunted, adding, 'Some people have all the luck!' before continuing to lead Mary along in the direction of the investigations unit, Iain walking with them, Mary eyeing him cagily, curious to see what his reaction would be to his friend's remark.

He remained strangely silent however, until, all necessary arrangements having been made, and leaving George McBrayne behind, he walked Mary back to the casualty department.

'Trust him to make cracks like that,' Iain muttered then, sounding aggrieved. 'He might be great at his job, but he can be very tactless. Don't let him embarrass you.'

You're the one who's embarrassed, thought Mary, noting his flushed face and thinking it plainly obvious that his friend had touched a raw nerve somewhere in him.

She was left with no time to speculate on the whys and wherefores, however, because upon reaching Casualty just then she was immediately immersed in teaching the new SHOs, and answering their innumerable questions.

She was even able to completely forget Iain,

which would have come as something of a relief
had she only had time to realise it!

The evening passed in a flurry of activity,
Andrew moving his possessions into his new
accommodation and Mary preparing the room for
Debbie-Ann's return. The twins were no great
help, although they tried to be, hauling Andrew's
cases into the porch—even if they did so before
he had them packed!

Finally, the room ready, Mary put the boys to
bed while Andrew drove to the airport to fetch
Debbie-Ann. At least, Mary attempted to get the
twins settled for the night but they were too
excited about seeing Debbie-Ann again and kept
coming out of their room to see whether she had
arrived.

Cuddling them, supporting one on each knee,
Mary asked them how they would like to be able
to play in the big garden behind the large gates
they had peered through.

At the mere idea their excitement increased
until it was impossible to hold them. Had it not
been already dark they would have been off to
the garden there and then, Mary was sure.

'You must visit the grandparents first,' she told
them, 'and promise to be very kind to little Emma
who has been very lonely and longs to have some
nice children to play with her in that lovely big
garden.'

'*We're* nice,' the boys said in unison, preening
themselves.

'Does Emma's nanny think you're nice, that's
more to the point.' Mary smiled wryly.

'What point?' Richie asked curiously.

'Never you mind,' said Mary, kissing him on the top of his head, which meant kissing Rob too, his head bowed in readiness.

'Well, come on,' she said, giving them further cuddles and affectionately ruffling their hair, 'back to bed, then we can tell Emma's nanny how obedient you are and that will please her.'

So the boys went back without further trouble, although at the first sound of Debbie-Ann's voice when Andrew brought her back from the airport, they sprang out again and rushed into the little lounge to greet her.

'You two should be asleep,' she declared, hugging them, 'but it's lovely to see you again!'

'Did you bring presents?' Richie asked, Rob echoing the question, his eyes, like Richie's, eagerly roving over her luggage.

'Now, now,' Andrew reprimanded them, 'you shouldn't ask things like that!'

'I'm not going to unpack until the morning,' Debbie-Ann said firmly, 'so you might as well go to sleep until then, and the sooner you go to sleep the sooner morning will come!'

So, although pouting and grizzling a little, they went off to their beds, Mary following to tuck them up and kiss them goodnight again. She was not looking forward to Debbie-Ann taking over from her again, having enjoyed being able to do some real mothering while she was away, Andrew having proved no rival in that respect. . .

She wondered whether he had heard the rumour linking him with the twins as their

night-time father and was glad for his sake as
well as hers that he would be seen to be sleeping
in his own flat from that very night onwards.

At first it had been quite fun having him to
stay, and he had certainly been very useful, but
as the days wore on he had shown a different side
of his nature, proving not to be as easygoing as
she had thought him at first. There was no doubt
but that his ways were not her ways, while the
unfounded jealousy he had shown towards Iain
had tended to spoil things quite often.

Even Gabrielle seemed to have cooled off in
her initial regard for him. Whether or not the
change in him had come about because he was
bored and frustrated, aching to get on with the
work he had trained to do yet having to wait a
full month before being able to get started, Mary
had no way of telling, for he always tended to
be uncommunicative about his feelings. . .being
much more inclined to joke his way around personal questions, avoiding giving in-depth answers.

Debbie-Ann was different too. . .or perhaps it
was. . .'Jet-lag and all that,' as she claimed. Or
maybe it's just me, thought Mary, acknowledging
to herself that she was growing sour, losing the
bubbling well of happiness she had once had permanently inside her.

Formerly she would have attributed its loss to
the deep sorrow occasioned by Robert's death,
but now she was more inclined to blame it on
her progressively poor health—not that she had
wanted anyone to know about that until circumstances had forced her to confide in Iain.

Creeping into bed later after cooking Debbie a
light supper, she felt very down, the worrying
business of the rumour adding disproportionately
to her other troubles until, unable to sleep, and
again in pain, she quietly sobbed the night away.

The next morning the boys' excited chatter
over-ruled all chance of her having any sort of
private conversation with Debbie-Ann before it
was time for the twins to be taken to their playgroup and Mary was due to join the casualty staff
in the Royal Glen.

'We'll talk later while the boys play in the park,'
she and Debbie-Ann promised each other before
parting, Debbie-Ann saying she would take the
twins to the flat and give them their tea first before
going to the park, to give time for Mary to join
them there.

A plan which served them well, for there was
a lot to talk about, Debbie-Ann wanting Mary to
hear not only the worrying news about her father's
condition but also the happier news that she had
met up with a former boyfriend, a young lawyer,
and. . .Debbie-Ann had tensed up with excitement while imparting the news. . .they had
decided to become engaged at Christmas when
he and her parents intended coming over to
Scotland for a short holiday.

'You'll like Peter, I'm sure,' Debbie-Ann said,
'and he's a very successful lawyer.'

'But what about Andrew?' Mary dared to
wonder aloud.

'He doesn't stir my blood as Peter can.' Debbie
looked surprisingly bashful. Mary had seldom

seen her show as much feeling before. 'Besides, my parents had always hoped Peter and I would make a match of it. They are his godparents, so you can guess how long they've been friends with his mother and father.'

'When do you plan to marry?'

'Well, naturally Dad wants to give me away, but his health is so bad now that I think he feels there is no time to be wasted.'

'So you'll be going back to the Cape with them after Christmas to prepare for the wedding?'

'Something like that,' Debbie-Ann answered, her eyes shining, then, a shadow crossing them, 'It all depends on how my dad is at the time, of course.'

So Mary decided not to say anything about her own precarious health. It was enough, she thought, for Debbie-Ann to have her father to worry about, so, glad for her that there was the thrill of the coming engagement to help her not to fret about him too much, she listened with obvious interest to all the rest of Debbie-Ann's news, saying little herself.

What love can do! she was thinking however, remembering how awkwardly uncommunicative Debbie-Ann had often been before. Now she was simply bubbling over as if unable to contain herself! Just as I was a long time ago, Mary sighed, suddenly feeling quite ancient compared to Debbie-Ann although the girl was only six years her junior.

She stared down at her own left hand. There was just the thin gold band on her wedding finger, no engagement ring. She had had to sell it in order to buy the extras needed when not just one baby arrived but two at once, born within minutes of each other. . .

She had never let her parents know she was in need of more cash in those early days, knowing that Robert would have wanted to supply all the children's needs himself.

She smiled, thinking of him, and the wonder he would have felt at being the father of two such bonny boys. . .

A wistful smile.

'Time to take the boys back for tea, I suppose,' Debbie-Ann suggested, running out of news. 'I'm going to miss them when I go back to SA.'

'And they'll miss you,' Mary said.

'Was Andrew much help?'

'Oh, yes. I couldn't have managed without him taking them to the playschool and bringing them back to the flat each playschool day. Did you know that little Rob had meningitis just after you left?'

Debbie-Ann stared at Mary, aghast. 'No! You didn't mention that in any of your aerogrammes!'

'I didn't want to worry you. It's all right to tell you now when you can see for yourself that he is fine again.'

'But. . .meningitis!' Debbie looked horrified.

'He was starting with it the night you left.'

'I told you he looked flushed and seemed unwell!'

'I know, I was aware of it myself so immediately contacted our GP, who gave him antibiotics and

Iain Stewart took him into the Royal Glen to have
him looked after, the Royal being nearer than the
Nightingale.'

'Oh, I wish I'd been here to visit him!'

'I was with him all the time except when
Andrew took over, or Iain. . .'

'How is Iain Stewart? Any less formidable?'

'He's all right,' Mary answered, purposely
casual. 'Come on, let's collect the boys from the
swings; I'm always scared they'll swing themselves
right off one day.'

'*Meningitis*!' Debbie repeated, finding it hard
to believe. But when walking across the playground with Mary she went back to talking about
her Peter, while Mary fell to wondering what she
would have to say about Iain's offer to allow the
twins to play in the gardens of the big house.

Would she read more into the offer than Iain
intended? Look for a romantic reason behind it?
How very disconcerting that would be. So she
decided to delay telling her for as long as she
possibly could, a plan which was soon foiled, Iain
calling round to the flat that very evening.

Fortunately he came rather late, which was just
as well, the twins having been far too excited by
the unpacking of the various new toys Debbie-
Ann had brought them to be able to settle down
to sleep until long past their usual bedtime.

Would Iain mention his proposal regarding
their use of his family's garden? Mary wondered.

And of course he did, almost straight away after
the usual pleasantries such as how did Debbie-
Ann enjoy her South African trip, what was the

weather like there, how were her parents and so on, even showing an interest in their state of health, which Mary thought was very polite of him, knowing he had never met them and how wearied he must be after a long day on the wards listening to the many descriptions of symptoms in other people's illnesses.

His relief when he could introduce the lighter subject of when and how the twins could be introduced to his grandparents, niece and nanny was apparent, and the question was soon settled. The next day being Saturday and neither he nor Mary being on duty, the decision was that they would bring the twins to tea at three-thirty.

Mary was the only one to show any doubts, but then she was the only one who knew how she was feeling, and how sick she had been during the night, sick and in a lot of pain.

'You would prefer not to come?' Iain asked, eyeing her discerningly. 'Shall we leave it for another time?'

'Oh, no,' she answered with an air of 'let's come and get it over'.

'You don't feel so good, do you?' he muttered quietly, moving over to her side. 'But a delay won't help, will it, so I think you are being wise to make all the arrangements you can as quickly as possible?'

'Are you all right, Mary?' Debbie asked, growing equally concerned. 'You look very pale and now that I've had a chance to really notice, you have lost an awful lot of weight while I've been away. Have you been skipping meals?'

Mary returned a rather feeble smile. 'No,
nothing like that,' she said. She looked towards
Iain with a questioning air, and he nodded as
if agreeing to her telling Debbie-Ann about her
swallowing difficulties, but before she could say a
word he made his farewells to both girls, and left.

'That was decent of him,' Debbie-Ann said. 'He
must have realised we wanted a tête-à-tête. He
can be quite nice, can't he? I can understand you
being a bit smitten with him. . .oh, sorry, there
I go again, I shouldn't have said that, should I?'

'No, you shouldn't,' Mary said quite severely,
and, rising from her chair, she put the kettle on
to boil, and waited in silence to make the tea,
not feeling particularly friendly at that moment
either towards Debbie-Ann or the world in general, in fact not towards anyone really. . .except
for her sleeping twins, of course.

Having let the tea brew, she poured out one
cup, pushed it towards Debbie-Ann and said with
an air of apology, 'Hope you don't mind if we
postpone our talk. I had a rotten night last night
and the lack of sleep has caught up with me. I've
just got to go to bed.'

'Goodnight then,' Debbie-Ann said. 'Sleep
well. I expect I shall, but I want to write to Peter
first. We promised each other we'd exchange
letters every day.'

'That's nice.' Mary hid the unhappy envy she
felt. It was a long time since she had been able
to write to Robert.

'Goodnight, Debbie-Ann,' she said with a
weary sigh. 'I'm sorry if I've been awkward

tonight, I'm just very tired, that's all. Oh, but
there's one thing I must ask you—does Andrew
know about Peter? Won't he be upset by
the news?'

'No. He won't settle down for years yet. Will
probably become a flying doctor in Australia—
that's his latest idea. He won't stay here long. If
anyone has itchy feet, he has. Besides, he falls
for every girl he sees, although I think he could
have been serious over *you* but realised Iain had
beaten him to it.'

A view which Mary would have questioned had
it not raised her secret hopes where Iain was concerned. Not that she allowed herself to
acknowledge them, but her dream when she
finally fell asleep was full of romance, and her
knight in shining armour was the very image
of Iain.

CHAPTER ELEVEN

'COME along,' Iain called to Mary, Debbie-Ann and the twins, on the Saturday afternoon as soon as he entered the flat, 'my folk await you!'

He seemed in jocular mood as he handed them into his family-owned Land Rover then drove them along to Beech Grove and up the drive to the big house.

'Hooray!' shouted the twins as Iain lifted them down from the vehicle, then, 'Emma!' they called delightedly, running as fast as they could to greet the little girl standing rather shyly waving to them from the top of the wide semi-circular steps leading up to the huge iron-studded front door.

'They certainly know one another,' Mary laughed as the boys awkwardly grabbed hold of Emma's hands and tried to lead her down the steps.

'They should do,' remarked Debbie-Ann, 'she's there at the playgroup most days. I had no idea she lived here though. Oh, look!' Her smile brightened as she caught sight of a smart young woman coming out through the door behind Emma. 'It's Anne, Emma's nanny. We became quite friendly when taking the children to the playgroup just before I went to the Cape. Come and meet her, she's nice.'

'And then come and view the children's playground,' Iain butted in. 'I've been busy equipping it for boys as well as girls.'

Mary turned on him. 'So you fully intended having my twins play here, without awaiting a decision from me either the one way or the other?'

'Now I've vexed you again!' Iain heaved a great sigh but looking at him Mary decided he was not taking her reprimand all that seriously, which annoyed her still further until, drawing her back away from the others, he muttered, 'Mary, Mary told me earlier that she was ashamed of becoming so ill-tempered. . .but did she mean it?'

The whole atmosphere improved from then on, Mary making an effort to be her old lively self, and Anne proving to have a quick wit and an easy way with children, cheerfully and tirelessly helping them test all the climbing frames, ropes and slides Iain had provided.

'See how soft the ground is beneath them?' Anne tested it proudly. 'Spongy, springy and bouncy! There's not much risk of the children hurting themselves even if they fall.' She smiled approvingly towards Iain.

That she liked him was evident from the way she kept referring to him, thought Mary, taking note too of the warmth in the glances she kept casting in his direction.

She found herself wondering what the relationship was between them, and the more she wondered, the more the pain in her heart sharpened. Iain had said he had never come across the girl he would want to spend his life with, then had added a whimsical, 'Well, not until. . .' and left the sentence unfinished. He must have been thinking of Anne, she decided, then wondered why that conclusion should bother her.

After all, Anne would probably make him an ideal wife, having all the attributes she herself lacked yet had struggled to acquire, but only for her Robert, of course.

Not wanting to think any more along those lines, 'Won't your grandparents be wondering why we haven't gone into the house to greet them?' she called to Iain. 'I don't want to stay too long,' she added.

He looked at his watch. 'The tea should be ready by now, so yes, we'll go in.' He smiled towards Anne. 'My grandparents' afternoon nap should be finished by now, don't you think? It's four o'clock.'

'Then come along, children,' Anne called, and to Mary's surprise the twins immediately came off the climbing frames, but whether because tea had been mentioned or they were simply acting in response to the firmness in Anne's voice, she had no idea.

'See that?' Debbie-Ann whispered. 'Maybe she'll be good for them, what do you think?'

'You don't do too badly in that respect either.' Mary responded albeit dejectedly, a mood of despondency again assailing her. 'I'm the only failure,' she muttered, not that Debbie-Ann heard; she was already hurrying on to join Anne and the children.

But, 'What was it you said?' Iain dropped back to walk with Mary. 'Why should you think yourself a failure?' he queried, looking puzzled.

Mary raised a faint smile. 'You weren't meant to hear my groan,' she said.

'You're not a failure,' he declared valiantly, remaining serious. 'Just think of all you have accomplished so far. You're downhearted because you have something wrong with you that you're not able to put right yourself. Something that makes you less than perfect in your own judgement, and you want to be perfect in every way, doctorwise, womanwise, motherwise, but sadly have been deprived of the chance to be a long-term perfect wife. Am I right?'

Although he slipped an arm around her she raised no objection.

'Just concentrate on getting your medical problem sorted,' he suggested sympathetically. 'You'll be surprised how much brighter things will seem when you are able to enjoy eating and look forward to having good meals again.'

After giving her shoulders a quick, comforting squeeze, he dropped his arm from her and they followed Debbie-Ann, Anne and the children up the wide balustraded steps to the huge oak door.

His grandparents welcomed them all and were so kindly both in looks and manner that Mary soon felt at home, while the three children, seated at their own special table away from the grown-ups, were served with the animal-shaped sandwiches, cakes and jellies the cook had obviously taken pleasure in preparing for them. Beaming, she bustled in, sat between the twins and the tea became something of a happy, if boisterous, celebratory party.

'Just look at Emma,' Anne murmured to Mary. 'She's doing her level best to keep up with your boys. I haven't seen her eat so well for ages!'

'I told you that you'd be doing us a good turn if you allowed the twins to come and play with Emma,' Iain maintained when back in the flat, having driven Mary, Debbie-Ann and the twins home from the big house. 'So let's hope it's the first of many visits. Well, I've to go now—on call all night tonight! Coming to the door with me, Mary? No, don't bother, I'll let myself out.'

To say Mary was surprised by his initial request was to put it mildly. She and Debbie-Ann raised eyebrows at each other, shrugged, but made no comment.

Working with Mary in Casualty a day or so later, however, Iain was back to his old distant self, so she lacked the impetus to tell him about the phone call she had received that morning. Her barium meal X-ray had been arranged for the coming Tuesday, the motility studies for the Wednesday and she was warned not to eat or drink anything on either of those two mornings.

'You never have breakfast,' Debbie remarked when told, 'so it shouldn't be a hardship for you, not like it would be for me!'

'Or for the twins!' Mary quipped back, doing her best to hide her fear of what she saw as a possible dilatation ordeal.

It was difficult for her to settle her mind to anything after that, although she carried on with her work in Casualty to the best of her ability in spite of Iain's unexpected reserve just when she felt a need to talk to him and get his reassurances.

Tuesday came and with it the barium meal X-ray, the barium swallow being carried out with her lying prone, then standing erect, in order to demonstrate and to ensure distension of the gullet. There was nothing unpleasant to put up with however, much to her relief.

But the motility studies carried out on the Wednesday entailed having a tube inserted into each nostril to register the pressures on the oesophagus, and what with those tubes and a clip over her nose registering her breathing pattern, she felt anything but a pretty sight when unexpectedly Iain walked into the room which at that moment was empty except for Mary.

To her relief he sensitively turned his back to her. 'I only popped in to suggest you take the rest of the day off,' he said, 'and as I've been able to arrange for our other Casualty consultant to take over from me I too am taking time off. . . Actually,' he hesitated, 'I wondered whether you would care to tour the Trossachs with me. . . would you like that?'

At first she simply nodded, then realising he could not see her response, she said a short, 'Yes, Debbie-Ann permitting. I'll phone her,' speaking in an unfamiliar but understandably nasal voice.

'Right,' said Iain, 'I'll be waiting.' Then he disappeared back out into the corridor and in spite of her acute discomfort Mary felt a strange joy at the prospect of having him to herself for a time to talk to and confide in once again.

Because all she really wanted was to be able to talk to him, she assured herself, knowing it wouldn't matter half as much if achalasia did turn out to be the cause of her swallowing difficulties and explain the now almost nightly coughing and choking sensations, as long as she could tell Iain all about everything and hear his views, and perhaps once again know the comfort of his arm about her.

'Achalasia has been confirmed,' she said as they motored around Stirling on their way up to the Trossachs. 'I've seen the X-rays and heard the results of the motility studies.'

'Well, try to put all that unpleasant business out of your mind for at least the next few hours,' he said disappointingly. 'Enjoy with me the wonder of the scenery. I'm going to take you up to the Bracklinn Falls where the Keltie Water beautifies and transforms giant rocks into glittering steps, while high above them trees of all shades of greenery, their leafy branches sighing and singing in the sunlight, cast magical patterns on the silvery waters in the deep gorge below. It really is an entrancing sight.'

'As entrancing as I appeared earlier on today?' Mary asked, testing to find out whether he had actually taken a look at her before turning his back when she was participating in the motility studies.

'I was careful not to look at you, wasn't I?' he reminded her, his face crinkling humorously. 'I knew you would expect me to adhere to a strict code of honour in such things!'

Mary dared not look at him; she could tell from the smile in his voice that he was trying to reassure her, but that he had caught a glimpse of her before courteously turning away. She decided to give him credit for trying to be tactful, then, thinking of the way she must have looked, her own sense of humour rekindled and she laughed.

Iain's response was immediate and dramatic. Stopping the car by the roadside, he gathered Mary in arms that seemed unable to wait, and before she realised what was happening he kissed her, gently at first then with gathering fervour.

'Don't!' she cried once or twice, but her voice carried no meaning and she showed no real resistance, so he kissed her again, and again until she was unable to stop herself responding. Then, releasing her, he sighed, a deep, rapturous sigh which she found herself echoing.

'I couldn't help myself, Mary,' he said apologetically after a few silent moments. 'I've been longing to hold you in my arms and kiss you ever since you I first saw you all those months ago in the regional casualty meetings.'

She sat quietly listening and trying to calm her heart down.

'You must often have thought I was mad with you, but the truth was that I was mad *for* you, believe it or not. Because you made no secret of your love for Robert, and I realised the depth of your sadness, I had to hold myself in check. It's been a very testing time.'

Still Mary said nothing.

'I know the sort of person you are,' he continued, his hands gripping the steering wheel, his knuckles showing white, 'and I realise that Robert. . .lucky man. . .will always come first with you, but that won't stop me wanting you for myself, as I do—oh, I do, Mary!'

He made to put his arm around her again but she edged away.

'You're angry with me, Mary? Because you couldn't help returning my kisses? You were wanting me just as I was wanting you, confess it now!

'Or were you pretending to yourself that it was Robert who was kissing you, loving you? Is that why you responded, Mary? I have to know! My desire for you is tormenting me, tearing my heart to pieces. . .I told you I have never before met a girl with whom I would want to share my life. . . well, I have now, and the yearning inside me is reducing me to begging for a return of love.'

Mary stirred, but kept her distance from him. 'Could we go on to Loch Achray now?' she asked in a very small voice. 'I need the tranquillity of its still waters, to feel again its healing serenity. . .'

'Of course.' Completely subdued, Iain started up the car engine. 'It was wrong of me to add to the pressures already being brought to bear on you,' he muttered after driving some distance. 'Please forgive me.'

Mary answered by resting a hand on one of his for a brief moment, her heart much too disturbed for her to be able to find words to express her feelings. . .not that she even knew what her real feelings were, she was so confused.

There was no denying that she had found herself welcoming his kisses, had even desired them. . .but why? That was something she was unable to figure out. Her love for Robert was as strong as ever; nothing had changed in that direction, so again. . .why?

It was a puzzle she was unable to solve. In the meantime, she told herself, she would have to keep Iain at bay, out of fairness to him, and to herself.

Nevertheless she was happy to have him hold her hand as they strolled through the beautifully wooded Crags to Loch Katrine for a glimpse of its lovely tree-clad islands, then, getting back to the car, they visited the Pass of Leny with its magnificent waterfalls, made their way back through Callander, along by the river Teith, where they invested in bags of stale bread and had fun feeding the ducks, then drove on back to their respective homes, all talk of love or romance very carefully and quite deliberately avoided.

Which was just as well, for Mary had more to think about than romance when an official hospital letter arrived the next morning telling her she was booked to see Mr George McBrayne, the gastroenterologist, in his outpatients clinic on the following Monday.

'Your friend George wants to see me again,' she told Iain later in the day, wanting him to know.

He nodded, and she guessed from the gravity of his expression that he suspected she was to be referred to the upper-gastrointestinal surgeon, the well-known and highly respected Mr Hirst.

She made sure she was early for her appointment.

'Then, as the surgeon in question was holding a clinic in an adjoining suite, Iain's friend George took me in there with my X-rays and results,' she told Debbie-Ann on her return to the flat, 'and they discussed and debated, finally deciding a balloon dilatation should be tried before proceeding to a major operation.'

She paused, still bravely smiling, then suddenly broke down. 'Oh Debbie-Ann, I'm frightened,' she said, her face crumbling. 'People expect doctors to be brave, but I'm not, I'm scared about the possible outcome of all this.' A tortured expression spoiling the clarity of her blue eyes, 'What happens to the twins if I don't recover?' she burst out, putting her dread into words.

'Don't recover?' Debbie scoffed. 'Recover from what, a balloon dilatation? You'll only be in hospital one night! Oh, Mary, you must be in a bad state of health or you would never be thinking the way you are.'

She appeared to be racking her brains to know what to say in order to help. 'I'm no preacher,' she said finally, 'but you know as well as I do that it's only when we're on our beam ends that we're given help from above, and you haven't even started to sink to your weakest level yet! Be patient, something will turn up.'

She stared around as if looking for inspiration. 'Wait until you find you have to have the major operation you have often said you'd hate to have. . .you'll think a dilatation a mere piece of cake compared to that, won't you? Then be grateful for small mercies and thankful you haven't to face the major operation.'

'I've tried to follow your advice,' Mary said to her a couple of weeks later, 'I faced up to the balloon dilatation, as you know, but food is getting more and more stuck, not less so. I think I shall have to take my courage in both hands and see Mr Hirst. This time I'm pretty sure I know what he'll say. . .he'll want me to have the Heller's myotomy, which might mean having to have my chest opened.'

'Spare me the details,' pleaded Debbie-Ann, 'or you'll make me scared too, and I've the boys' breakfast to see to, and a picnic to pack!'

Mary's smile was tremulous. 'And I've to give them their good morning hugs,' she said, making for their bedroom and wishing with all her heart that she could go on the picnic with them. She didn't want to leave them; Debbie-Ann couldn't know what a wrench it was going to be to go into hospital and not know what was happening to them meantime. She didn't know if she could bear it.

When Iain called in on her later that evening she told him she had point-blank refused to have a major operation so soon.

'You can't do that!' he gasped, scandalised and remaining standing. 'Why do you make things so awkward, Mary?' he frowned. 'To comply would be to your benefit, surely. You're taking a terrible risk with your health.'

She chewed at her lower lip, her eyes downcast. 'Well, you weren't here when the landlord. . .'

Her voice dropped until it was almost impossible to make out a single word she was saying.

'The landlord what?' Iain was positively bristling.

'Caught me as I was coming home, and with a face as dark as an impending storm gave me notice to leave,' Mary mumbled. 'Complained about the twins, the noise, the mess they make, the way they sometimes kick a ball against downstairs windows, the water forever spilling from our bathroom into the one beneath. He went on and on. And he blocked my path. I couldn't move out of his way. It was all pretty horrible.

'He yelled that he'd warned me until he was blue in the face, and he wasn't going to lose any more tenants because of two mischievous little kids who wouldn't do as they were told.

'I'm afraid I snapped back. I was livid, especially when he gave me two weeks' notice to get out of the flat.'

'I'll talk him round,' said Iain.

'No, I don't want to stay. It's the unfriendliest place ever. . .and it was what he ended up saying that really got me.' Mary started to colour up. 'And you wouldn't want me to stay, not if you knew what he'd said when he turned back.' Mary seemed too uncomfortable to repeat the landlord's accusation.

'Tell me,' ordered Iain in his perfunctory manner.

Her colour rose. 'Do I have to?'

'Please,' Iain urged more gently.

'Said I'd given the house a bad reputation. Two men coming in at all hours of day and night, he shouted—what did I think anyone would think? I should know better, he said, and since I've no regard for the welfare of the other tenants I had to go otherwise the police would close the house down and they'd all be out on the street.'

'And what did you answer?'

'You'll think me terrible,' she watched him closely, fearing his disapproval, 'but I couldn't help it, I made use of the cold, stinging tone I keep for rebutting false accusations and declared I'd leave not in two weeks, but one.

'Then I had to rush to get to work on time. I longed to tell you what had happened, but knew you were off for the day. . .'

'Wanted to tell me—why me?' Iain looked pleased, nevertheless. Then, more thoughtfully, he added, 'It didn't occur to you to placate the irate man just to gain extra time for a move?'

'No, not after the awful things he'd said. Besides, he had no intention of letting us stay a moment longer than necessary, I could see that written in his eyes, read it in his face.

'Then I thought, supposing the fault lay with the tenants; after all they could have complained to me instead of running to him!'

Iain looked grim. He had hardly moved.

'But finally,' said Mary, 'I came to the conclusion that the main blame lay with me. I've been so incredibly naïve. No doctor should be as naïve as I've been, especially not one who has been so romantically involved as I was with Robert, bearing him two children. But somehow, because I knew that Debbie-Ann and I wouldn't. . .oh, you know what I mean. . .I expected everyone to realise that too, no matter how bad things looked for us.'

'Well, we will have to do some hard thinking,' Iain said, 'but now I really do have to go.' He walked over to her, placed a light kiss on her forehead and left.

At work the next morning he discovered her hiding away in a corner of Casualty, surreptitiously wiping her eyes. Sympathetically he attributed her tears to fears about the operation.

'I don't think I'm thinking that way,' Mary disagreed, going on to remind him of her altercation with the landlord. 'I feel so guilty because I'm putting Debbie-Ann, the twins and myself out of a home. What was I thinking of, to allow such a thing to happen?'

Impatiently she again wiped a handkerchief across her wet eyes. 'It seems to me I'm growing thoroughly nasty, making enemies out of those who were once friends,' she claimed miserably.

'You're under stress,' Iain pointed out again. 'I'm sure everyone realises that.'

'It would be good if everyone thought as you do,' Mary gulped. 'But the truth is I'm putting backs up all over the place. The nurses, porters and even the young doctors are wondering why they never seem to be able to please me any more. I see it in their eyes and hate myself, yet I don't seem able to correct the intolerant impression I'm giving.' She paused to wipe her eyes yet again.

'And now there are the twins to worry about,' she continued a moment or two later. 'What is to happen to them if they have no home to go to and I'm laid up in hospital? What do I do? Leave my bed and walk the streets with them all night, every night?'

'Now you're not thinking straight,' Iain reproved her firmly. 'They'll be taken care of, you'll see. Debbie-Ann and I already have plans in hand, knowing your operation is set for Tuesday.'

'Tuesday? How do you know?'

'James Hirst mentioned it to me.'

'Before telling me?' Mary burst out angrily. 'That's a bit off, isn't it? Besides, I thought I'd postponed it for a while?'

'You can't do that, you need it! Anyway, when do you have to leave the flat—did the land-lord say?'

'He gave me two weeks' notice but as I told you, I was so angry I said we'd be out in a week.'

'You don't make things easy for yourself, do you?' Iain frowned thoughtfully. 'Well, look, I have some urgent paperwork to see to. Debbie-Ann and I will sort everything out. Have the operation and get well again—that's your job for the immediate future.'

Debbie-Ann and I, Debbie-Ann and I. . .the words ran through Mary's brain, repeated all day long. How close were they? she wondered anxiously, then stopped herself, sure she was being foolish. Nevertheless she couldn't help wondering whether he knew that Debbie-Ann was supposed to be getting engaged at Christmas? Shouldn't someone tell him?

'No. . .no. . .no!' a voice cried inside her. 'Don't interfere, you've enough difficulties as it is!'

So she simply avoided Iain, even when he came in towards the end of her day.

The next morning another official letter came from the hospital, this time telling her she was to go in at ten o'clock on Tuesday morning for the major operation scheduled to take place at half-past two the following day.

Now what? thought Mary miserably. . .what am I supposed to do with the twins? I haven't been given enough time to make any alternative arrangements, let alone find a permanent second home for them! Or even another temporary home, come to that!

Asking Debbie-Ann not to say anything to the boys about the enforced eviction, in case it gave rise to fear and uncertainty in their minds, Mary was nevertheless relieved to have Iain call in that evening, and while Debbie-Ann busied herself in the kitchen with the twins, she took the opportunity to ask him to tell Mr Hirst why she had to postpone the operation and make her excuses for her.

'I certainly won't do anything of the sort!' Iain said firmly. 'You need the operation and the sooner the better. Mr Hirst is going on an overseas tour starting next week, training doctors in developing countries to do the operations he specialises in. He's one of the best in the world they say; that's why I wanted him for you. Trust me, Mary, I'll see that you and the twins are OK.'

'But there's nothing you can do! Rented accommodation is virtually non-existent here, especially if children have to be catered for. I know, for didn't I search high and low before I found the flat I've just lost? No, it's my fault, I should have been more careful in what I said to the landlord, then he might have let us stay. My temper is always getting the better of me now.'

'You're having a lot of problems piled on you these days, so don't blame yourself too much!'

'Then who can I blame?' Mary's chin quivered insecurely.

'Me, for instance?' Iain gave her a quizzical smile.

Touched, impulsively she drew closer to him, reaching out to put a tentative hand on his arm.

Covering it with his own, he stroked it gently, even lovingly.

'Seemingly you're the one person who really cares about what happens to the boys and me,' she murmured, 'or so I'm beginning to think. Thank you, Iain.'

She lowered her eyes, fearing she had become far too emotional to meet his gaze without betraying the unexpected feelings suddenly so insistently overwhelming her heart.

CHAPTER TWELVE

It seemed to Mary that before she had had a real chance to get to grips with her new job as staff-grade surgeon in the Royal Glen's Accident and Emergency department, she was being forcibly sidetracked into having to have the major operation.

What would the health authorities be thinking of her? she wondered. Would they begin to doubt whether she was up to the job? Consider her health could not stand up to it, or feel the wrong person had been chosen? She could hardly blame them if they did.

'I wonder what Robert would have made of all this palaver,' she burst out to Debbie-Ann when they were on their own after getting the boys to bed. 'It's horrible not being able to talk to him about it. Oh Debbie-Ann, I do miss him so. I reach out to feel him beside me when I'm half-asleep at night sometimes, expecting him to be there. . .then I——' she was unable to continue for a time '——I realise he isn't there, he never will be there again, and my heart nearly breaks. . .'

'It seems to me,' Debbie-Ann replied thoughtfully, and in her rather blunt way, 'that you do tend to dwell on the loss you suffered by his death rather than concentrating instead on the wonderful happiness you shared with him while he was alive. Don't you think that's a big mistake on your part?

'Surely you don't intend carrying a torch for him all the rest of your life,' she went on in increasing earnestness, 'completely ignoring the fact that your boys need a father figure to look up to, and have never known what it is to have one? Shouldn't you be putting them first, before your own grief, and trying to find someone who will ably fulfil that paternal role, help them to have a stable, disciplined yet loving home life, guided and guarded in a way you can't manage, not being male?'

She looked surprisingly awkward, then continued as if forcing herself, 'Oh, I wouldn't blame you hating me for saying all this, but I must. I care so much for you and the twins and want to see you all happy and living fully rounded lives. Please try to understand what I'm getting at.' She hesitated. 'After all, there *is* someone who would make a wonderful father for the twins, they all get on so well together, and you and he seem a little in love already if you ask me!'

Mary waited, the light of battle in her blue eyes. Was Debbie-Ann suggesting she should let someone replace Robert in her heart?

'Iain Stewart,' continued Debbie-Ann, greatly daring. 'He could be the right one.'

'I think you've got it wrong there!' Mary stormed, provoked and exasperated, and hurrying to get away to her own room. Once there, she found herself studying her empty bed and for a

moment blushingly picturing Iain lying there
beside her.

Then her thoughts returned to Robert and for
the first time she allowed herself to wonder what
he would think—would he be in favour of his
sons having another man to call 'dad', another
father figure as Debbie-Ann put it, a man to help
protect their welfare?

Knowing the sort of person Robert had always
shown himself to be, she had no doubt but that
he would want whatever was best for them. But
what would be the best? How was she to know?

Perplexed, early as the evening was, she
undressed and got into bed, then lay there admitting to herself that the very thought of sharing
her life with Iain tempted her more than she had
ever dreamt possible, whereas, should they part
and never see each other again, she would, she
knew in a moment of deep revelation, regret it
for the rest of her life.

In the morning, 'Sorry if I deserted you last
night,' she said apologetically to Debbie-Ann,
'but I needed time to think. All your fault.' She
smiled forgivingly nevertheless, then continued
pensively, 'Your words of advice tossed and
turned in my mind the whole night long. I just
didn't know which way to go or what to do for
the best.'

Debbie looked at her wan face and sighed. 'At
least that means I took your mind off the fact
that you're going into hospital as a patient today,'
she said. 'The twins and I will pop in to see you
later this evening and bring along anything you've

forgotten to pack to take in with you. But Mary,' she added as if on an afterthought, 'what exactly is achalasia? I've never heard of it before.'

'Well, if I gave you the proper medical description I don't think you would be any the wiser,' Mary said woefully, 'not unless you understand what failure of the mechanism producing relaxation of a sphincter leading to dilation and muscular hypertrophy of the part immediately above the sphincter, oesophagus in my case, means,' she replied, giggling a little at Debbie's flummoxed expression.

'Shouldn't have asked, should I?' Debbie pulled a wry face. 'But what does that actually mean?'

'Well, in almost plain English it means that the muscles of my oesophagus are unable to push food downwards and the sphincter or ring of muscle at the entrance to the stomach fails to relax to allow food through.'

'So what will the surgeons be doing to you?'

'Well, I thought it was to be another balloon dilatation to stretch the sphincter muscles so much that they tear and can't work so food can fall through instead of getting stuck. But Mr Hirst thinks that as I'm young he'll have a greater chance of success this time if he operates laparoscopically, you know. . .keyhole surgery. . .so that he can cut the offending muscle under direct vision rather than tearing it with the balloon.'

The strange thing was that when Mary reached the Royal Glen to be clerked-in and have all the necessary pre-operation tests, the very first person she came across was Iain.

'You're early!' he exclaimed. 'That's good. I wanted to talk to you while you're still conscious.' He spoke in humorous vein, cupping her elbow with his hand and hurrying her along. 'We've time for a very quick tea in the canteen, so come on, I've something important to say—have been watching out for you to arrive.' And to Mary, who had been digesting Debbie-Ann's suggestion all through the night, it was almost as if Robert had arranged for them to meet. She faced Iain shyly.

'I wanted to relieve your mind of worries about your future accommodation,' he began, vigorously stirring his sugarless black coffee and appearing apprehensive about the effects his next words might have.

'All my personal things have been moved out of the Gate House,' he rushed the words, keenly watching her face, 'and it has been thoroughly spring-cleaned all ready for Debbie-Ann and the twins to move in. I think they'll find it quite comfortable. So will you when you leave hospital, I'm sure. There are three bedrooms.'

Mary sat gaping in surprise, her coffee forgotten. Then his news began to sink in.

'And you, where will you live?' she managed to ask.

'Oh, I'll be in the big house.'

Of course, nearer to Anne. . .that thought hit her immediately.

'You don't look too pleased with the arrangements,' Iain remarked, 'but honestly, we all thought them the best we could come up with.'

'But why wasn't I consulted?' Mary asked, aggrieved. 'Did you all take it for granted I would veto your ideas?'

'Something like that,' he said frankly. 'You're in no fit state to think anything is good news, which is understandable considering the circumstances. However, there was no alternative, Mary. . .not for love nor money could anyone find any more suitable accommodation.' He paused. 'Perhaps I shouldn't say "not for love", for love always finds a way, as on this occasion, doesn't it?'

The gold flecks in his hazel-brown eyes seemed to dance as he teased. 'But, not to digress,' he continued, sobering down, 'at least you'll know where your boys are, have them well looked after by both Debbie-Ann and Anne with lots of room to play in safety, out of doors and indoors, plus a nice little companion in Emma, my grandparents keeping a watchful eye on all three youngsters. I'll be around quite often too—daytimes only of course!'

His smile was so disarming she just had to smile back.

'You're sure you're not angry?' He rose to his feet.

She shook her head, her expression sweetening.

'Then——' He looked around, saw no one was watching, and stole a quick kiss before hurrying away, muttering as he went. 'Be good and do everything you're told to do, forget to be stubborn.'

Typical! thought Mary, piqued, but her heart

softening towards him all the same, then, almost as if compelled to do so, her fingers covered her lips as if to press the kiss to her, while at the same time a few tears rolled gently down her cheeks, her emotions being in such confusion.

The rest of the day was nothing if not trying. After collecting her notes from the Admissions Office Mary went up to the surgical ward only to find there was no bed available for her, which meant her having to wait in a smoke-filled day-room worrying because she knew that hours spent in passive smoking could have an adverse effect on one's breathing during an operation, and for her twins' sakes even more than for her own, she grew more and more anxious.

It didn't help her sinking spirits when a woman came and sat beside her loudly complaining about doctors. 'I'm fed up with them,' she grumbled. 'I've had a bowel preparation and now I've been told there's no bed so I'm to go home and come back tomorrow. . .then go through it all again, I'll warrant! Doctors give us unpleasant treatments then have no sympathy! They should become patients themselves and be made to take a dose of their own medicine—that would learn them!'

'Is Dr Macgregor here?' asked a young houseman at that moment, poking his head around the door. 'I've to clerk you, Doctor,' he explained when Mary rose. She blushed guiltily, frustrated in her attempt to keep her medical identity secret, and went out with the houseman to the accompaniment of an embarrassing gale of laughter.

To her relief, however, a bed had been found for her so she had no need to return to the day-room; instead she was able to unpack, change into her newly bought blue-spotted white satin pyjamas with matching dressing-gown, and lie down.

Later, having been checked by the anaesthetist, then vetted by the cardio-respiratory technician who did an ECG, and afterwards seen by the senior registrar on his ward-round, she felt she was well on her way towards the operation.

Much to her disappointment, however, she found it was not scheduled to take place until the next day. There was little to do but wait, although Debbie managed to call in for a few minutes but without the twins.

'I've left them with Anne,' she explained, 'she's very capable. Iain is on call tonight, did you know? Road traffic accidents are keeping Casualty very busy.'

Inexplicably disappointed because she wasn't to see him, nor the twins, Mary found the night passing very slowly. The surgical ward was very busy too, and incredibly noisy, one patient forever getting into the wrong bed, two patients coming up from Intensive Care, others being sick, and drinks trolleys and medicine rounds effectively preventing Mary from getting any sleep.

However the night proved quite an eye-opener to her, one that, in a way, she was glad to experience. Being a doctor, she was offered a side room, but refused it, preferring to stay among the patients she was getting to know and to value for their cheerfulness, humour, kindness towards each other, and sheer bravery in the face of what was often intense suffering.

In the morning her hospital chaplain visited her, bringing the Sacrament of the Sick, and stayed chatting for a while afterwards, otherwise it was a time of simply waiting and observing, a very tedious morning, Mary's operation having been postponed again, this time to the afternoon, which meant having to stay 'nil by mouth' all those extra hours.

Finally, however, the surgical consultant came to see her, followed a little later by some lively joking porters, who, together with an escort nurse, pushed her, still in her bed, down to Theatre.

And when the operation was over at long last, and she had fully awakened from the anaesthetic followed by a shorter more normal sleep when back in her ward, her pain relieved by painkillers, she opened her eyes.

Her vision still being rather blurred, she sensed rather than saw someone standing by her bed.

It was Iain.

'Debbie-Ann and I have brought the boys along to say a brief goodnight,' Iain said. He sounded harassed and worn, as if he had been worrying. . .

Openly taking hold of her hand, he gently stroked her fingers one by one, then tenderly smoothed her fair hair away from her damp forehead. 'Don't try to talk; your throat must have been roughened by the endo-tracheal tube. All we came for was to see for ourselves that you're OK after that long operation. You gave us all a fright,' he added, his face strained and serious. 'We thought you were never coming out of that operating theatre. Six hours there instead of the expected two and a half! The trouble was, your abdomen had to be opened. A laparotomy. Oh, that nerve-racking waiting, but—my dearest dear, what joy to see you now!'

At which point Debbie-Ann discovered that the twins had disappeared!

So tucking Mary's hand back under the sheet, Iain went in search of them, eventually finding them down at the far end of the ward where, having decided to cheer everyone up, they were visiting every bed, even those in which the occupants were already asleep!

'Fortunately they haven't disturbed anyone who objected to being disturbed,' Iain said with relief, delivering them back to Mary's bedside. 'However, I think we'd better take them away before our luck turns,' he added, wiping his perspiring brow and grabbing the boys firmly by their hands. 'They were about to worm their way back by crawling under the beds!'

'We're hurrying 'cos Emma's nanny's making supper,' Rob let out in his loud whisper.

'When will we be old enough to eat 'dult's suppers, Mummy?' Richie asked, his blue eyes wistful as he stretched to lean over her bed towards her.

'Shush.' Debbie-Ann pulled him back. 'When

you're old enough to open tins of baked beans,'
she replied for Mary, remembering her previous
dictate.

'What a criterion by which to judge ability!'
Amused, Iain lifted the boys one at a time to
plant a goodnight kiss on Mary's cheek, enjoining
them to be very gentle.

'Now it's my turn,' he said, bending over her
still form and kissing her on the lips again. 'See
you tomorrow,' he murmured. 'Have a good
night, Mary. . .now we really must go.'

She tried to turn towards him, but her operation
wounds prevented her from moving, and she
moaned a little.

'Stay still,' said Iain. 'Don't make yourself more
sore than you need be.'

And Debbie-Ann stayed back for an instant to
whisper, 'Did you hear the affection in his voice,
Mary? I told you he cares for you, didn't I?' Then
she and Iain led the boys away just as Andrew
rushed into the ward, a long box tucked under
his arm.

'Hello, goodbye!' he said to them as he passed.
'Mustn't stop; I've only just made it in time!'

Finding Mary's bed, he leaned towards her
before looking back over his shoulder as if to
make sure Iain was watching, then, walking round
so that she would be facing him, he laid the box
beside her with a flourish which might or might
not, have concealed a kiss, it was impossible to
tell, and, opening the box, he drew out about a
dozen beautiful red roses.

'From you?' Mary mouthed, still a little dazed,

although pleasure wreathed her pale face at the sight of the flowers.

'Me?' Andrew shook his head. 'No, I'm still trying to clear my debts! Actually a nurse handed them to me to pass on to you when I asked if I could just have a quick peep into the ward, visiting time over notwithstanding. I haven't a clue who sent them, but it's your name on the box right enough. Isn't there a card?'

He searched the box. 'Nothing,' he said. 'Never mind, now we know I'm not the only one who loves you! Well, I'd better dash before I'm thrown out! See you again soon, Mary. Get well quickly. Bye!'

And with that he was gone, leaving Mary to sink back into her pain-killer-induced doze to dream that Robert had been to see her, bringing flowers.

When she awakened the next morning there was another box of beautiful red roses waiting by her bedside.

Again no card, and Mary was too painfully immobile to even look, leaving it to Debbie-Ann and Iain to try to unravel the mystery when they popped in during visiting time that afternoon.

A few days passed, a fresh bouquet of red roses arriving every day and being shared around the ward, the up-and-about patients placing vases containing some on every locker, although still the mystery remained unsolved as to why and from whom they had come.

'Anyway, I love them, so does everyone around, and they make a good talking point,'

Mary told Gabrielle when she paid a surprise visit.
'I thought you were still on holiday,' she added,
'not due back until the weekend!'

'You're a lot brighter than you were a week or
so ago,' Gabrielle smiled, not offering any explanation of her unexpected return. 'It's good to see
you getting back to your old form.'

'Full of the joys of spring?' Mary quipped.
'Even if my spring came a little late this year!
You can't guess how wonderful it is to be able to
eat and enjoy eating once again, even if my diet
has to be a little restricted for the moment. . .
And, do you know, Mr Hirst, my surgeon, said
today that it's now up to me to decide when I'll be
fit to leave hospital, so I told him I'll be departing
tomorrow!'

'Oh!' Gabrielle seemed a little dropped-on by
the news, and broke away from Mary rather
abruptly, leaving her puzzled and wondering why
the sudden haste.

She was to find out the next day, when instead
of Debbie-Ann coming to help collect up her
belongings for her as had been arranged,
Gabrielle arrived again instead.

There was a terrible thunderstorm raging over-
head at the time; nevertheless Iain came with his
car to take them to the Gate House, where he
left them as he had to return to Casualty.

'Where are the twins?' Mary asked, nervous
for them, knowing they might be frightened of
the storm.

'The nanny up in the big house has them playing
with her charge—Emma, isn't that the little girl's

name?' Gabrielle said. 'We'll get you settled first, then I'll phone and inform the folk up there that you're here. In case you're wondering, I came back early from my holiday in Killarney especially to take over from Debbie-Ann.'

'Why?' Mary asked, puzzled, knowing Debbie-Ann had been coping well.

'Because she's been recalled to Cape Town. Her father's had a stroke and naturally her mother wants her support and company. Debbie-Ann received a cable yesterday and got in touch with me. She said she had seen you but hadn't had the heart to tell you, but personally I think it's best for you to know exactly what's happening.'

'I agree, but oh, poor Debbie-Ann. You know, I thought she was being a bit close-lipped yesterday. I do hope her father makes a good recovery. But why didn't Iain tell me when he visited me last night? Oh, of course, he was only able to stay a moment or two, being on call.'

But he stayed long enough to kiss me goodnight, Mary could have added, had not Iain's kisses begun to mean more to her than she would want anyone to know.

'In any case he would probably have thought it best to leave it to me to tell you,' Gabrielle was saying. 'Now, let's get you into bed. Would you like anything to eat or drink?'

'Not at this moment,' Mary said, as an earthshaking clap of thunder seemed to shiver the very timbers of the little Gate House. 'I was always told to keep away from water taps and even things like telephones while there's lightning around.

'Will you be staying here tonight?' she added a little wistfully, obviously hoping the answer would be a yes, because she had no wish to be left on her own.

'Of course,' Gabrielle smiled understandingly. 'I'll stay and share your room tonight and Mr Stewart will bring the boys down from the house, and will stay here himself, using Debbie's room, if the storm continues. Anyway, that's what he actually suggested himself.'

'All these big trees around make me nervous,' Mary murmured.

'I know, they are a bit threatening,' Gabrielle agreed.

So, the storm continuing, Iain came, helped Gabrielle put the twins to bed, and stayed the night. Mary, seeing and hearing him around, was able to get the feel of having him in a house with her. It was a comforting experience. She was quite surprised. Not even the continuing rumble of thunder accompanied by incessant vivid flashes of lightning and the creaking and groaning of the overhanging trees was able to worry her.

But when, the storm abating by morning, Iain drove the boys up to the big house to play with Emma, then dropped Gabrielle off at the Nightingale Hospital, leaving Mary alone for those few minutes, she suddenly felt lost in loneliness.

She was fully dressed by the time he returned. 'I've to hold a ward-round at eleven,' he told her. 'Would you like me to take you up to be with Anne, Emma and your boys?'

'Your grandparents might not want me there,' she replied diffidently.

'They might not even see you; they'll be supervising the packing being done for them. This is the time of year they go up to their Highland home for a spell. As for not wanting you, why do you think they've insisted on me taking you up to the Highlands to convalesce?'

'Just me?' Mary asked in surprise and some alarm.

'No, they wouldn't dream of expecting you to separate youself from your twins, neither would they wish to deprive Emma of the company of her new playmates. Anne will be going along too, to help keep an eye on your progress healthwise, and I have a couple of weeks' holiday due, so you'll have plenty of company, and a real chance to get fit enough to return to work within the prescribed six weeks' sick leave. What d'you say?'

'I don't think I have much option either way,' Mary said. 'My parents can't come over until Dad's early retirement papers come through, and as the boys and I have been turned out of the one and only flat I was able to find after much searching, I'm sure we're unlikely to find another in this locality, so. . .?' She shrugged her slender shoulders high in a hopeless gesture, then winced, her operation scars objecting to being stretched.

'And you'll be without Debbie's help,' Iain reminded her for good measure, at the same time grimacing as if sharing her pain. 'It seems to me that you are going to have to rely on Anne to assist with the boys.'

Mary turned her head away to hide a sudden spate of jealousy. Anne seemed to be taking over her twins as well as Iain himself. Or was she letting her imagination run riot?

'So that's settled.' Iain stood up. 'As soon as you feel fit enough we'll travel up to Glencoe either by helicopter or by car, whichever you think you'll find the most comfortable. You won't have any work to do, so let's go as soon as we can. Gabrielle is due back on duty next Monday, she tells me, so we could give her a day or two up there with us first, to make up for the holiday she cut short to help you out.'

'Good idea,' Mary nodded, determinedly pushing unworthy sentiments aside, ashamed of allowing herself to get jealous of Anne who was so helpful. 'But where would we all stay?' she asked.

'In my grandparents' home. It's a big rambling place, outwardly similar to one of the old Scottish castles—you know, turreted, but modernised inside without losing any of its original charm and character. You'll like it, I'm sure.'

'I love this little Gate House,' Mary said pensively, 'and the old-world cottage garden surrounding it. Who tends the garden, by the way? Do you? I've never seen so many beautiful red roses!' She eyed him suspiciously, the canny gleam in her eyes throwing down a challenge.

'Not even in those boxes of roses you received?' Iain asked, glancing anywhere but at her.

'It's a wonder you have any left,' Mary remarked, watching as a guilty blush infused his cheeks.

'You're too astute, Mary,' he claimed. 'It was to be my secret. You see, I tried to act as I thought Robert might have acted and came up with the romantic idea of having red roses speak to you for me, telling you of my love. And I do love you, and long for you. The yearning never lessens, never. . .it's become one big ache inside me, tearing at my heartstrings all the time.'

'Robert was no gardener,' Mary said gently, 'you were wrong about that. Nor was he romantic in the way you mean.' She studied her clasped hands. 'Passionate, yes, but not romantic. Those two characteristics don't always go together. Sometimes I could have wished. . .' She looked up at Iain, her eyes brimming over with tears. 'But what's the use of wishing? Robert was as he was, I am as I am, and you are as you are.

'And Iain——' Her voice dropped, becoming almost too quiet to hear. 'Don't try to change. I like you as you are.'

'Like?' He reacted to the word by reaching out to her impulsively, holding her very carefully, yet very close. 'Is "like" all you feel, Mary? Does "like" explain your response to my kisses? I don't believe it! I think you love me. I don't know why you should, but I know you do. And what's more, I think Robert knows you do, and approves, having learnt to be as generous with his heart as he was with his life. After all, do mothers and fathers love their last child any less than their first? No, and why not? Because hearts are made to stretch to encompass all, equally.'

'Thank you,' Mary whispered against him, 'I

hadn't known how to love you without being disloyal to him, but now you have made the way clear. I can love you both but in different ways, it's as simple as that, isn't it?'

'The trouble is, I'm greedy—the day will come when I shall want his share as well as my own.' He looked down at her and smiled tenderly, but there was something in his voice that excited her and made her tremble in spite of her attempts to remain placid and calm.

'However,' he added, his handsome face crinkling into the crooked smile she now found so attractive, 'that can wait. What we have to do first is build up your strength again, and organise that get-together party you so wanted to have.'

'You mean it?' Mary's eyes shone. 'And there'll be room for everyone? Where, the big house, and grounds—weather permitting?'

'Of course. And we'll add a special celebration of our own, a wedding reception! O Mary Mary, you'll make such a lovely Christmas bride, and the little Gate House you love will be our very first real home together, for you will marry me, won't you? Say yes, if only to help put an end to the rumour the twins instigated about having more than one dad coming and going at all hours!'

'So you've heard about that?' Mary couldn't help giggling.

Tenderly gathering her closer, Iain kissed her, then kissed her again and this time Mary put a hand up and around the back of his head to draw it closer, irrespective of the pain the movement caused her sore frame.

'Marry you?' she whispered. 'Oh, Iain!' And she sighed, nestling contentedly in his arms.

'The one and only dad, that'll be me,' he said huskily, 'no matter how many sons or daughters you might have eventually.'

'But I'll want to keep on with my career as well,' Mary insisted.

'Of course. That's where Anne will come in handy; she'll be in her element as a loving, caring nanny to all our children, growing old with them, bless her!'

It seemed that nothing could repress Iain's unusually high spirits. Looking down at her, he held her carefully close. 'And when you are completely fit again and the Glencoe mountains are clothed in their dazzlingly white mantles of snow, we'll take a real holiday, a second honeymoon, and go skiing. Oh, but can you ski? If not, I'll teach you.

'Oh, Mary, I'll teach you so many things. You can't guess how I'm beginning to appreciate the sweetness yet forthrightness of you, your face so often reflecting humour, your cute little nose, smooth line of chin, oh, all of you, everything about you is beginning to attract me. . .the sharpness of your mind, your ability to answer back, your honesty, your great love for your twins, loyalty to your Robert, yes, even your dreaminess and the way you can act as young as your sons or as mature as any of your patients or doctors. . .'

'Well, I don't know about that,' Mary chuckled, 'but I do know that despite your many shortcomings. . .'

He blew out his cheeks in mock resentment. 'Cheeky talk like that deserves to be punished,' he said, kissing her again, and again. 'Oh, Mary,' he murmured when he could, 'and to think I once likened you to a silent unstirred pool of still waters. . . .'

'"With hidden depths to be probed", wasn't that what you said you found tempting?' Her eyes were beguiling, her smile inviting. 'But now——' she looked up at the cuckoo clock on the wall '—you'll be late for your ward-round if you don't go straight away.'

'Oh, heck, so I shall!' Iain gave her another tender hug and still with the gold flecks in his eyes dancing with joy and delight in the promise of future happiness, he rushed out to his car, waved an answering kiss to her at her window, then sped back to the Royal Glen hospital.

Meanwhile Mary studied the wedding photograph now gracing the beautifully carved wooden mantelpiece in the delightful lounge of the Gate House. Focusing her gaze on Robert and thinking also of Iain, she found it wonderful and quite incredible that she should have won the love of two such fine men.

And that afternoon the playschool had its sports day, so Iain collected her to go and watch the twins taking part.

'Richie is the school's athlete,' he chuckled. 'I wouldn't want us to miss this for anything in the world. I've seen him practising!'

The sprint was just starting, and as expected, Richie was soon out in front, but every time he realised it, feeling sorry for the losers, he turned and waited for them to catch up before he actually began running again.

Iain and Mary gripped each other, collapsing on the grass with laughter, the whole thing was so hilarious, then, the race over, both twins ran to them.

'It's the dads' race next,' they cried, struggling to pull Iain to his feet and push him towards the miniature race-track.

'They've got the right idea!' he said, winking at Mary, then, tucking a twin under each arm, he ran, and won.

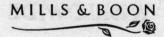

NORA ROBERTS

◆

SWEET REVENGE

Adrianne's glittering lifestyle was the perfect foil for her extraordinary talents — no one knew her as *The Shadow*, the most notorious jewel thief of the decade. She had a secret ambition to carry out the ultimate heist — one that would even an old and bitter score. But she would need all her stealth and cunning to pull it off, with Philip Chamberlain, Interpol's toughest and smartest cop, hot on her trail. His only mistake was to fall under Adrianne's seductive spell.

AVAILABLE NOW   **PRICE £4.99**

W🌓RLDWIDE

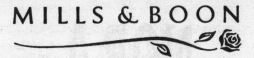

MILLS & BOON

LOVE ON CALL

The books for enjoyment this month are:

STILL WATERS Kathleen Farrell
HEARTS AT SEA Clare Lavenham
WHISPER IN THE HEART Meredith Webber
DELUGE Stella Whitelaw

♥   ♥   ♥   ♥   ♥

Treats in store!

Watch next month for the following absorbing stories:

NOTHING LEFT TO GIVE Caroline Anderson
HIS SHELTERING ARMS Judith Ansell
CALMER WATERS Abigail Gordon
STRICTLY PROFESSIONAL Laura MacDonald